T0207905

Cancer & the Lottery

Ally's Way, the Last Letters

Brinton Woodall

authorHOUSE®

AuthorHouse™
1663 Liberty Drive
Bloomington, IN 47403
www.authorhouse.com
Phone: 1 (800) 839-8640

Published by AuthorHouse 01/18/2016

ISBN: 978-1-5049-7377-9 (sc)
ISBN: 978-1-5049-7376-2 (e)

Library of Congress Control Number: 2016900852

Print information available on the last page.

Contents

Part Two: The Last Letters

Ally's Way

$\diamond\!\times\!\diamond\!\times\!\diamond\!\times\!\diamond\!\times\!\diamond\!\times\!\diamond$ Part One $\diamond\!\times\!\diamond\!\times\!\diamond\!\times\!\diamond\!\times\!\diamond\!\times\!\diamond$

Ally

*T*he last time I wrote in my book, it was exactly one year, four months and three days ago. So much has happened to my new sisters and me. Janice took me in until I turned eighteen, and then I bought a condo that overlooks Central Park. Janice bought a home forty-five minutes outside the city, and Sarah and Melinda bought a condo on the east side of the city and are roommates. We usually meet on the first Saturday of each month to catch up.

I love it when we all visit. They always make my day. There's nothing *like people caring for you when they have no agenda behind it.*

They help me escape any problems that someone my age goes through.

When it comes to my mother, it bothers me that we do not get along, and that she relapsed back into her addiction a few months ago.

It hurts me to see her like this. I begged her numerous times to stop, but I realized she will never change. Her pain is no longer physical, it's mental, and I can't blame her. She lost my sister, her daughter.

However, this still does not give her the right to be the victim. I should be the victim. I was a ward of the state, not her. Marisa used to beg her to stop, and then she emancipated herself and never looked back.

I hate to open these wounds that have not been able to heal, but if I don't, then who will? I need therapy to get through my issues, and because I don't feel comfortable telling anyone, this notebook will have to do for now.

We can thank Professor Morry for this choice of therapy.

Ally

Professor Morry

S itting in professor Morry's class, Ally can't help but think of her sister, Marisa.

She sits in the same seat that her sister used to sit in when she attended Professor Morry's class.

Professor Morry says,

"Our ongoing assignment for the last month of class will be to use a marble notebook to write down your most intimate thoughts about what you are going through inside and out. You don't have to come to class, so I hope we can try the honor system where you write down your thoughts and feelings. You never know what can come from doing this for a month. A few years ago, a young student of mine passed unfortunately, but kept her thoughts and writing and it became a best seller.

We all have a story in us, and this month you're going to write that story. Now that I have you all ready to go to sleep, class is dismissed."

All the students start to head out, except Ally, as Professor Morry ask her to stay after class to talk.

Professor Morry came up and asked, "How are you, Ally?"

"I'm alright, I guess."

"Are you sure you're just alright?"

"Yeah, why do you ask?"

"You don't have the same spirit that you showed in the beginning of the school year. Is there anything you want to talk about?"

"Nope, and if there is, I'll be sure to write it all down," Ally says with a sarcastic smile."

Professor Morry grins and says,

"I'm looking forward to hearing your story. Your sister loved you. It's all in her writing. She always thought about you. Every personal note was about her love for you and wishing she had the courage and strength to help rebuild a relationship with you."

Ally says to Professor Morry,

"Maybe that's the problem. She only wrote it down. She never took the time to tell me why she felt that way. So to me, as much as I do love her, they are only words. So with that said, have a great day."

He smiles and says,

"You too, Ally."

Issues at Home

Ally now heads to her mother's apartment to check in on her.

The elevator is not working, which aggravates her. She takes a deep breath to distract herself from thinking about the flight of stairs she has to walk up.

As she is walking up, she comes up behind an older woman who is walking very slowly, which wears Alley's patience very thin.

It is a lengthy fifteen-minute walk up the stairs, although it would have only taken five minutes if the elderly lady hadn't been moving as slow as molasses.

Exhausted, Ally walks gingerly to the door, and knocks lightly. A man comes out of the apartment, looks at her, and then begins to walk down the flight of stairs.

Assuming the worst Ally rushes into the house, and calls,

"Mom, where are you?"

"I'm in here."

"Where is here?"

"The bedroom, I think."

Ally rushes in and sees pills all around her mom's bed, and her mother lapsing in and out of consciousness.

Ally rushes her mother to the bathroom, turns on the shower, and hopes that the water will wake her up.

She says,

"Wake up, wake up! Why do you always have to do this?"

Her mother does not respond to the question, just smiles, and says,

"Because."

"Because what, because what, what?" Ally screams frantically.

Ally continues,

"I'm tired of this. I can't do this anymore. I refuse to deal with you. I should leave you like you did your other daughter."

Her mother looks back at her and says,

"I did not leave your sister. Your sister left me. She emancipated herself, which made the state take you. So don't blame me. Blame her, damn it. Blame her."

Her mother starts to cry, and Ally gives her a hug as both of them stand in the tub.

Ally turns on the shower to help her mother shake off whatever is happening to her. As the water falls, Ally starts to hum and sing softly to her mother. It's her own rendition of the child's rain song.

She says,

"Come on mom, lets sing that song you used to sing to us. I'm going to remix it a little, okay?"

Ally's mother nods her head. However, she just listens to Ally singing the song.

Her voice cracking, she begins to sing to her mother,

"Here we go: *Rain, rain, go away. Don't be ashamed. Rain, rain, go away. My love for you will stay the same. Rain, rain, go away. Stop bringing all this pain my way. Rain, rain, go away.*"

She repeats this to her mother a few times until her voice becomes weak and her mother's weight becomes heavy on her chest. Ally turns off the running water and carries her mother to her bed. She finds a pair of sweats in the hamper, shakes her head, puts them on, and walks out of the house to head back to her place, as she is supposed to meet her sisters to pick the four locations where they'll go on their new adventure.

Bucket Hat

All of the girls are waiting impatiently in the hallway for Ally to come home.

After a few minutes of huffing and puffing, Ally shows up in the dingy sweats, trying to fix her hair a bit while talking to the girls, her keys dangling out of her backpack.

Sarah asks,

"You okay?"

"Yeah, I'm good. Why do you ask?"

Janice says,

"Because you're wet, as if it rained today."

Ally looks at Janice with a face so cold that if Janice touched her hand, she would be cut.

Ally says,

"Move out of the way so I can open my door please. Thank you."

The girls all follow Ally into the house, take off their shoes, and sit in her beautifully furnished living room, which has a three-piece couch in a rich mahogany brown.

The girls complain that their feet are cold, so Ally walks over to the front door, where there is an electronic key pad. She presses a few buttons to turn on her oak wood-heated floors; then she starts her fireplace, and opens her window, where Central Park's great lawn lays in view.

While they talk and catch up, all the girls are writing down different locations for their infamous annual vacation. They have over a hundred locations to choose from.

Ally says,

"We need a hat."

Sarah replies,

"Okay, so where are we going?"

Melinda, with her smart remarks, says,

"Aren't you listening? She needs a hat, and you're wearing one: not just any hat, but that ridiculous bucket hat."

For some reason, Sarah is still having a blond moment. It takes awhile for her to respond, but eventually the light bulb in her head clicks on and she says,

"Oh, okay, my hat, oh, you need my hat here."

The girls still wait for Sarah to give Ally her hat.

Finally, Melinda snatches the hat off Sarah's head, and a few strands of her hair along with it, which causes Sarah to yelp.

"Ouch, Melinda, that really hurt."

Melinda says,

"It wouldn't have if you took off your hat when Ally asked you too."

"Whatever, no reason to be so rude."

All the girls jump in to defend Melinda.

Ally says,

"Well, she does have a point."

Janice agrees,

"Yeah, she kind of does."

Sarah's eyes pop in disbelief that they all would take Melinda's side.

"Whatever. You guys are wrong. Let's pick these places, because I don't like you guys ganging up on me over my bucket hat, which I paid for. Shoot, get your own hat."

Ally shakes the hat, which is filled with numerous choices of vacation places. Janice is the first one to pick. She says,

"Alright, here we go," dips her hand into the bucket hat, and picks London.

Janice is so excited, she slides across the polished oak floor to think that they are going to London.

She starts to make up her own song about London, but realizes she is getting carried away when all the girls stare at her as if she needs to see a psychologist.

Janice smiles and walks back over to see what Sarah picks.

Sarah closes her eyes as if she is making a wish before she picks a country. She digs her hand into the hat and comes out with Costa Rica.

Sarah's choice makes her happier than a baby in a barrel of titties, even happier than a chubby kid finishing her favorite piece of dessert.

She says,

"Okay, before I dance like Janice, it's your turn, Melinda."

Melinda dips in both her hands and pulls out two destinations. She tells Janice to pick the left or the right. Janice goes along with Melinda being silly. She points at her left hand and starts the nursery rhyme,

"Eeenie, meanie, miney, moe, catch a piggy by his toe. If he hollers, let him go, eeenie, meanie, miney, moe."

Janice's hand lands on Melinda's right. She opens it and does not want to look at what it says.

Melinda tightens up her shoulders.

"Where we heading?" she asks anxiously, waiting for Janice to answer.

"We're going to Ireland, Melinda."

Melinda does not seem to be very enthusiastic about her choice. Her face shows utter disappointment, as if she has just been blown out in a championship game.

However, although she feels this way, she knows she will feel a lot better when they play a prank.

Now it's Ally's turn. She dips her hand into the hat and the last pick is Japan.

Ally puts on a brave face in front of the girls. Japan is somewhere she never wanted to go again, as it was where Marisa wrote that she wanted to go, as well as being the final place where they scattered her ashes.

Janice says,

"Yes, Japan."

Ally replies,

"Yeah, Japan."

Janice sighs.

"Oh Ally. Hey, we don't have to go to Japan if you don't want to. It's okay, really. It's not that big a deal. We understand if you don't want to go."

Ally forces a smile and plays with her hair before she says anything.

"Japan will be good for us. I need to go; as a matter of fact, we all need to go."

The girls agree with the sentiment and each of them is to write down all of the information needed for Ally to make the reservations for their trip.

Janice says,

"Alright, we'll all meet at the airport around three tomorrow."

London

The girls arrive at the gate and wait to board the plane. Sarah is anxious to get the show on the road, and starts pacing back and forth in front of the girls.

She's talking a lot and not saying much of anything: a lot of context, but not much content.

"I'm so excited. I can't wait to see all these places we're going. Why am I walking back and forth so much? Hey, Melinda what was in the canteen you gave me?"

Melinda says,

"Please do not tell me you drank the whole thing."

Sarah says,

"Yeah, I thought it was soda, although it was a bit sweeter than I expected."

Melinda shakes her head before she tells Sarah,

"That's because it's not soda, Sarah! There were three energy drinks in that canteen and you drank it all. I asked you to hold on to it, not drink it."

Janice tells her,

"I think you need to sit down now."

Although she wants to continue to pace up and down the aisle, Sarah knows Janice has her best interests at heart, so she takes her advice and sits down.

"Now that you said that, I feel my heart coming out of my chest."

Janice is annoyed. She has to deal with this, but is determined not to let this be a moment that ruins her day. She tries to salvage Sarah just before they board the plane.

Janice asks Ally,

"Ally, can you please get some water for Sarah so we won't have to deal with this forever, especially on this flight. I just can't, she is too hyped to sit on a plane for all those hours."

Ally says,

"Yeah, sure, give me a few minutes. I have to make a call real quick."

"Okay, that's fine."

Ally takes her cell phone out of her back pocket to call her mother and see how she is doing.

"Hello? Hello, mom? Are you there? I can't hear you. I hear static, Are you there mom, mom?"

"Yes, I'm here. Sorry, I have you on speakerphone. I'm washing some dishes. What's up?"

Ally tells her,

"Nothing much. I just wanted to let you know that I'm leaving town for a few weeks."

"Why, Ally, you know I need some money for groceries. You know my fridge is empty."

"No, Mom, it's not. Check your fridge. I filled it up when I put you back in the room.

"What? Let me check. Okay, but I don't want ham, I wanted turkey. That's why I told you to leave me the money for the groceries."

Ally is frustrated from trying to take care of her mother, so she keeps the conversation short before she gets emotional, and has to tell her friends what's wrong.

"Okay, mom, I'll make sure I leave you the money from now on, instead of doing you the favor of putting food in the fridge."

"It's okay, sweetie. Hey, you think you can give me some money for some clothes and to go to the movies?"

"I'll see what I can do, Mom. I'm gonna go now, my flight should be boarding soon."

"Okay, baby. Just send it to me. I really need it."

"Alright. Bye, mom."

"Bye, baby."

Ally walks to a fast food restaurant and buys a few bottles of water for the girls, but most importantly, for Sarah.

Ally rejoins them and gives everyone their bottles of water.

Janice says,

"Thank you. Sara is talking way too much."

Janice opens the bottle of water for Sarah and makes her drink all of it.

Sarah tries to say something, but before she can get a word out, Janice shoves the other bottle of water in her hand.

Janice says,

"Shush. Don't talk, just keep drinking."

The loudspeaker makes a crackling noise before the gate attendant speaks.

"Good morning, ladies and gentlemen. In just a moment, we will be boarding for the international flight to London City Airport."

Melinda says,

"That's us. Let's go."

They board the plane, take their seats, and the flight attendant tells them,

"Ladies and gentlemen, welcome aboard flight number 1589 to London City Airport. Please make sure that your carry-on items are stowed either in an overhead compartment or completely beneath the seat in front of you. If you have problems with the proper stowing of your items, please let a flight attendant know, and we will be happy to help you. If you are seated in an emergency exit row, please read the information on the passenger safety card that is located in the seatback pocket in front of you. If you do not meet the criteria for sitting in this row, or if you do not wish to assist in an emergency, let a crewmember know at this time and we will be happy to reseat you. Prior to departure from the gate, all cell phones must be turned off and stowed. Once again, we welcome you aboard flight 1589."

The girls recline their seats to enjoy life in first class.

As they wait for the flight attendant to come around to take their beverage requests, Ally takes out her notebook to write.

There are times when I love this lifestyle that my sister allowed me to have.

Then there are times when I absolutely hate it. Having financial security is a great feeling, especially since I never had that as a child growing up.

I always had my sister until she emancipated herself, which required her to tell the courts what was really going on at home: my mom's addiction to pills because of an injury at work, and how we only ate at school, so we would rush there to catch the morning breakfast program.

My mom always left it for Marisa to do that. I can't even remember my mom being sober, except for the first month, when Janice became my guardian and took me to see her.

Mom was so sweet that day. She made an amazing dish of chicken and steak with yellow rice and a green salad.

It was simple, but it showed me that she wanted to try, and I appreciated it. She has a good heart, just a poisoned brain that makes her feel she needs these drugs to be her best self.

It really sucks to see your mother not be able to kick a bad habit, and all you can do is watch, although you know you can't fight for her. Only she can do that.

Losing Marisa has been hard on everyone, so to be selfish and act like it only affected her is wrong.

My sister was the only thing I had to look forward to once I was old enough to leave the group home.

I hate leaving my mom all by herself, but I know I need some time away from trying to be her mom when she should be mine.

I hope I can relax a bit and enjoy some of the sightseeing we have planned in London and leave these thoughts of my mother right here in this notebook.

Ally

With the direct flight to London, they arrive in three and a half hours. After they go through customs and collect their luggage from baggage claim, they take a cab to the Royal House Guards.

The Royal House Guards is a beautiful, five star hotel that looks traditional from the outside, but is modern inside.

The girls open the door to their suite and find a basket of fruit and a bottle of red wine. They run to the bathroom and put on the plush robes there, so that they feel like royalty.

After a few hours of lounging around their suite, they decide to look at a few brochures to see what the city has to offer.

Sarah asks,

"You guys see any places you want to go?"

Melinda replies,

"I'm sure the Tower of London is a must."

Sarah asks,

"Is the Tower of London okay with everyone?"

Ally says,

"That's a start. After we go there, we can figure out what's next."

Melinda replies,

"Sounds like a plan."

Janice says,

"Stop talking and let's go."

The girls begin to feel a bit at home, as they wave their hands to stop a Hackney. It takes only five minutes for Melinda to lose her patience and blow a fuse, so she speeds up the process of stopping a cab by jumping into the middle of the street.

As the Hackney stops, the driver screams,

"What are you trying to do, kill me?"

Melinda replies,

"No, we need a ride."

"Alright, hurry up, get in. You're already in the middle of the street," the driver replies irritably.

Melinda ushers the girls into the vehicle, then slams the door shut and smiles. The driver looks back at Melinda in disgust.

"Where are you heading?"

Melinda tells him,

"We're going to the Tower of London."

"Okay, no problem. Please do me a favor and be gentle. I just cleaned the vehicle."

"Are you calling us dirty?"

"No, I'm calling you dirty in particular. You're a rude American."

Before Melinda can make a retort, Ally interjects,

"I'm sorry for my friend. I apologize. Can we just have a peaceful ride to our destination?"

"Sure we can. In fact, we're here."

After a short drive from the hotel, they are already in front of the Tower of London, and realized they could have walked. The girls are amazed by the beauty of the Tower. They thought it would not be that exciting, seeing how dingy and grim it looked from the outside, but they were so wrong.

The girls paid for a personal tour by a man named Niles, who is very well mannered. Niles is six feet tall and so slim you can easily mistake him for a number two pencil. He is very knowledgeable, as the history of his homeland is a passion of his.

He tells them,

"Thank you for visiting the Tower of London. Let me give you a brief history before we go into the details of this historic castle. The Tower of London was the home of the Royal families for many years.

There are twenty-one towers in the castle overall.

Melinda, being her feisty self, challenges Niles instantly on his knowledge of the towers.

She says,

"Oh, really? How many towers?" but as Niles starts to name them, she turns to the pamphlet to see if he says all the names that are listed.

Niles, shocked to be put on the spot, looks at her, and says,

"Are you serious?"

Melinda replies,

"Yes, very. Please start."

Niles smiles cockily, as he finds it amusing to be challenged by Melinda. Niles goes through the list of towers faster than a speeding bullet.

"If you insist on me naming all the towers, that's fine. they are The White, The Bloody Tower, Beauchamp tower, Bell Tower, Bowyer Tower, Brick tower, Broad Arrow, Byward, Constable, Devlin, Deveraux, Flint tower, Martin Tower, the Middle, St. Thomas, Salt tower, Wakefield, Wardrobe Tower, Well Tower, and last, but not least, the Lanthorn Tower."

Melinda tells him,

"I guess we can say that was impressive."

Janice says,

"Give credit where credit is due, Melinda. That was very impressive, Niles. Sorry she tried to challenge you."

"It's quite alright, Janice. Well, according to the package you guys paid for, you can observe four Towers. Which ones do you want a personal tour of?"

The girls all look over Melinda's shoulder so they can choose the places they want to visit.

Janice says,

"I'm choosing the White tower."

Melinda says,

"I'm choosing the Brick tower."

Sarah answers,

"Mine will be the Bloody tower. Ally, those are the ones we want to see. We can skip the fourth. By then we should grab something to eat."

All the girls are now inside the White tower and they look around and see how meticulously everything is placed.

Ally asks,

"Niles, who built the White tower?"

Niles says in his professional tour guide voice,

"Well, the Towers were built by William the Conqueror around the late 11th century. The White tower is the most important building in the Tower of London, because this tower alone is meant to secure every other part of the castle."

Ally, who is extremely engaged by the Towers, continues to ask questions.

"Niles, can you tell us what the tower's main function is or was?"

He replies,

"The White tower's functionalities were that it became the main base for the City of London. Supplies and horses were kept in this tower. If you look over to your right here, you will see the rooms they used to frighten the indigenous population of London. This was the tower where the Royal family would come in times of civil disorder as well."

Ally says,

"Wow. Can we check out more of the rooms?"

Niles replies,

"We usually don't." But then he hesitates.

"I'll make an exception, though. Follow me. I can get in trouble, so please don't touch anything."

Ally says,

"Thanks so much. Come on, guys."

Niles shows them three rooms and tells them quick facts about each room. The girls take a few photos and then continue on to the other towers.

The girls are in a buggy that Miles uses to drive them to the Brick Tower. As they walk up to the castle, Niles is already spouting an abundance of knowledge about the Tower.

"The infamous Brick Tower was built by King Henry the III, and it was completed in 1272. At one point, this tower held a prisoner by the name of Sir Walter Raleigh."

Janice asks,

"Who's that?"

"Sir Walter Raleigh? You're joking me, right?"

Janice shakes her head.

"Oh my, you're serious, aren't you?"

Janice looks at Niles and says,

"Yes, very much so."

"Walter Raleigh was everything from the sun to the moon: aristocrat, poet, and writer. He was also a soldier, a politician, and even a spy."

Melinda, who is not very impressed with Sir Walter's resume, says,

"That's it? That's all he did? I think he could have done a lot better than that."

Niles reaches a boiling point, and just wants to leave the Brick Tower. He is disappointed that they never learned about Sir Walter Raleigh, as they were taught so much about The United States, and yet they don't know anything about his culture.

He tells them,

"This man is the reason why some of your states have the names they do, like Virginia."

Melinda says,

"Okay."

"Let's just continue with the next tower."

They all make their way to the Bloody tower.

Niles tells them,

"We are not allowed in, so I will talk about this tower from out here."

Sarah, a bit taken aback, asks,

"Why not?"

Niles replies,

"Because."

"Because what? Something usually comes after because."

Niles says simply,

"It's haunted."

"Yeah, right."

"Like I said, no one is allowed in here except those who help with the upkeep."

Melinda then joins the conversation between Sarah and Niles, and says,

"You think that's something we would care about?"

Niles smiles, and then starts to talk about the Bloody tower.

"The Bloody Tower's original name was the Garden Tower. The name change took place in the 16th Century, when Richard, Duke of Gloucester, sent two Princes, one of them his own brother, to this tower, where the princes mysteriously disappeared. Rumor or legend has it that Richard killed both men; one was suffocated, the other was stabbed. The ghosts have been seen by many of us who have worked here, as well as the ghost of Sir Walter Raleigh, who was imprisoned in both the Brick Tower and the Bloody Tower. He's been seen inside as well."

Ally says,

"Wow, yeah, thank you for not letting us in there. I am definitely not interested in seeing some ghost."

She tells Niles,

"Thanks for the tour. I'll speak for them. I really appreciate your knowledge of the Towers you took us to see."

Niles replies,

"You're welcome. Enjoy the rest of your stay in London, ladies."

The girls then walk off the complex to go back to the hotel until it's time for dinner.

Ceviche

The girls are discussing where they should go to eat. Sarah wants some kind of seafood, but wants something light that will be an experience for them all.

She says,

"I want seafood, but nothing heavy."

Ally replies,

"Yeah, I sure can use a bite."

Janice says,

"Let's go to the restaurant 'Ceviche'."

Melinda asks,

"'Ceviche'? What's that?"

The girls let Sarah explain.

Sarah says,

"Well, ceviche is a seafood dish mostly popular in the coastal regions of Central and South America. There's a place in London actually called 'Ceviche,' and in this restaurant in particular, we get to make the food."

Melinda looks at all the girls and says,

"I want you all to know this is the dumbest idea ever. We're paying to make our own food?"

Janice replies,

"Yes, and we can actually use this because we're single. We all have homes and maybe only use the stove three times a month."

Ally interjects and says,

"Correction: I used the stove four times a month, not three."

Janice says,

"That's exactly the reason why we're going to this restaurant. So we can learn to cook a dish that's complex, so we can impress a man, or even better, impress ourselves."

All the girls start to laugh as they realize how pathetic they are, and how difficult it would be to date themselves.

The girls walk into 'Ceviche,' where they are met by a handsome gentleman named William. William is tall and slight, with somewhat Spanish facial features. The girls are in awe, as they thought he was the host, but instead he's the chef.

William says,

"Hello, ladies. Welcome to 'Ceviche,' where we teach you how to make ceviche. Today, I will be your personal trainer and show you how to make our world- renowned dish. On each of your respective tables, you will see the following ingredients."

William tells them each ingredient and holds them up as he speaks.

"Okay, you all should have bay scallops, limejuice, diced tomatoes, green onions, green bell pepper, a few stalks of celery, half a cup of parsley, fresh ground pepper, a little olive oil, and last, but definitely not least, a bit of fresh cilantro."

The girls look to see if they have all of the ingredients that William just described.

He begins to become more attractive to the girls, except to Melinda, who still can't believe they are paying to make their own food in a restaurant. William tells them what makes a great ceviche, and twenty minutes later, the only one with a delicious presentation is Melinda.

The woman is struck stupid looking at William.

William tells them,

"Rinse the scallops and place them in a medium-sized bowl. Pour limejuice over the scallops. The scallops should be immersed completely in the juice. Chill the limejuice and scallops until the scallops are opaque. Empty 1/2 of the limejuice from the bowl. Add the tomatoes, green onions, celery, green bell pepper, parsley, black pepper, olive oil, and cilantro to the scallop mixture. Stir gently. Serve this dish in fancy glasses and let's put this lime on the side of the cup for effect."

Everyone's but Melinda's dish looks like a dog would pass on it.

After making the dish, the girls all take a seat together to eat their ceviche. Melinda scarfs hers down as if she has been on an island for days and this is her first meal since.

Sarah says,

"Hey, we leave London in two days. We need to devise a plan and pull off a prank."

Melinda says,

"I agree, but on whom?"

Janice says,

"I don't know. Everyone has been nice. Who should we prank?"

Just like her sister Marisa, Ally knows she has an impeccable eye for whom to prank.

The girls suggest random people who crossed their path, until Ally has an idea that would be too challenging for any other prankster, but not for them.

Ally says,

"We're going after the palace guard. We're going to make them run off their posts just by throwing water balloons at them."

Janice says,

"Really? Water balloons?"

Ally tells her,

"Not just any old water balloons, pee balloons."

Janice asks,

"Pee balloons?"

"You heard me: pee balloons."

Melinda says,

"I know the best way to do this."

Janice asks,

"How?"

Sarah says,

"Drive by, duh."

Melinda says to Sarah with a smirk,

"I'm so glad you're getting to know me now."

All Sarah can do is smile and she's glad she isn't the slow one in the group, as that award went to Janice for this brief moment.

Ally says,

"Alright, girls: let's go back to the hotel. It's time to prep."

Sarah is awkwardly excited, and says,

"Yes, somebody is about to get pissed on," and then she starts rubbing her hands and makes a face that could get her thrown into a mental institution.

Janice leaves the money on the table, and the girls laugh at Sarah as they leave the restaurant and head back to the hotel room.

Operation Pee Guards

All the girls are drinking a lot of water so they can have enough of their special resource to fill up the balloons.

After hours of constantly drinking water to fill up each of their own personal bowls to pee in, the girls start to fill up the balloons with half of their urine and half water. They each have five balloons.

Ally tells them the plan in more detail.

"Okay girls, here's the plan. We're going to wear all black. I need Sarah and Janice to rent two cars. They need to be identical. I'm thinking a black truck, the best one available. I'm going to be the driver of one and I need Janice to drive the rest of you, cause I'm going to throw my balloons first, and then once the guards try to rush me, you girls drive your car while I drive off, and we'll have them off their post where we can really attack them."

Melinda says,

"That sounds good and all, but what about the license plates."

Sarah says,

"Dang, we forgot about that."

Ally says,

"No, we didn't. We'll screw off the plates and put them back on five blocks from the car rental service. Okay, that settles that. Let's go."

The girls are now all dressed in black; they have the targets in their sight, but Sarah, who is nervous, and afraid of the repercussions, starts praying. Ally, who knows her so well, speaks into the walkie talkie, as she is in her own vehicle,

"Is Sarah done trying to be a saint with her praying, so we can hurry up and pull this stunt off?"

Janice responds,

"Yeah, she just finished," and then she says

"Are you ready 'sour apple'?" which is Ally's code name.

Ally says,

"More then I'll ever be, 'caramel apple.' Operation Pee Guards is a go."

Ally drives as fast as she can after she says the word "go." She is wearing a ski mask as she stops the car and throws all the balloons, which could be mistaken for basketballs because they are so full.

She then drives off. The guards see something coming their way and one of them screams louder than any girl ever would. The guards are furious, and rush towards Ally as she hops back into the car. Lo and behold, Janice and the girls then stop the guards who are trying to chase Ally on foot in their tracks by hitting them with their balloons and then taking off.

One guard says,

"What is that smell? Did they hit us with water or urine, mate?" Both of the guards smell their jackets and say simultaneously,

"Its bloody piss!"

The girls rush the cars back to the rental center and continue to laugh about the prank they pulled off on their last night in London.

Ally says,

"That has to be the best prank ever, if I do say so myself."

Janice replies,

"Yeah, your sister would be proud of you, kiddo."

Ally asks,

"You think so?"

Janice says,

"I know so. You made up the prank last time we used her book."

Ally says,

"I guess that's true. Let's pack our bags and get ready to be on the jet tomorrow"

Janice smiles, and says,

"Alright. Costa Rica, here we come."

Costa Rica

The girls are excited to be on the jet to Costa Rica, and are all sipping champagne, except for Ally, who is looking at the Wikipedia page. She reads aloud,

"*Costa Rica, meaning 'rich coast' in Spanish, officially the Republic of Costa Rica (Spanish: Costa Rica or República de Costa Rica) is a country in Central America, bordered by Nicaragua to the north, Panama to the southeast, the Pacific Ocean to the west, the Caribbean Sea to the east, and Ecuador to the south of the Cocos Island.*

Costa Rica was sparsely inhabited by indigenous people before it came under Spanish rule in the 16th century. Once

a backwater colony, since attaining independence in the 19th century, Costa Rica has become one of the most stable, prosperous, and progressive nations in Latin America. It abolished its army permanently in 1949, becoming the first of only a few sovereign nations without a standing army. Costa Rica has consistently been among the top-ranking Latin American countries on the Human Development Index (HDI), ranking 62nd in the world as of 2012.

In 2010, Costa Rica was cited by the United Nations Development Programmed (UNDP) as having attained a much higher level of human development than other countries at the same income levels, while in 2011, the UNDP also identified it as a good performer in environmental sustainability, with a better record on human development and equality than the median of the region.

Costa Rica is known for its progressive environmental policies, and is the only country to meet all five criteria established to measure environmental sustainability. It is ranked fifth in the world, and first among the Americas, in the 2012 Environmental Performance Index. In 2007, the Costa Rican government announced plans for Costa Rica to become the first carbon-neutral country by 2021, and The New Economics Foundation (NEF) ranked Costa Rica first in its 2009 Happy Planet Index, and again in 2012. The NEF also ranked Costa Rica in 2009 as the greenest country in the world. In 2012, Costa Rica became the first country in the Americas to ban recreational hunting after the country's legislature approved the popular measure by a wide margin."

After hearing a bunch of boring facts about Costa Rica, Melinda says grumpily,

"Really, that's it? That's really what you just read?"

With a puzzled look, Ally says,

"What do you mean?"

Melinda replies,

"Why would I ever care about their ranking?"

Janice interjects before words that cannot be taken back are exchanged over a Wikipedia page.

"Okay, okay, we get it, Melinda. Thank you. Ally, can you please tell us some things that we can do in Costa Rica?"

Ally says,

"Sure, let me scroll down here. Ah, okay, here we go. In the City of San Juan, the capital of Costa Rica, we can go rafting, take a coffee plantation tour, and their national parks are considered to be some of the best in the world."

Sarah says,

"That sounds good. We're only here for three days and four nights. It's our shortest trip of all. Do you have a hotel picked out?"

Ally says,

"It's your destination. What are you thinking?"

Sarah takes a second and then says,

"I'm thinking of something relaxing, but not to the point that we don't want to leave the hotel, so let's do the Hotel Presidente. That's what I heard about on one of those traveling abroad channels."

Ally says,

"Okay, we'll book it when we land."

Hotel Presidente

The Presidente hotel in San Juan is amazing, and the view of downtown makes all the girls want to embrace their own city the same way the locals do in Costa Rica.

The girls check into their hotel room, which reminds them of their own homes. The women are all lounging in the living room, relaxing, until Melinda strikes up a conversation.

"What should we eat? I think we need to eat."

Janice tells her,

"Stop saying 'we,' and start saying 'you' need to eat. I'm fine."

Melinda says,

"Like hell. I saw you ask the flight attendant for seconds."

All the girls start laughing. Sarah is laughing so hard she starts to roll around on the floor. Ally is holding her stomach because of the way in which Melinda's quick wit has left Janice stuck for a moment, not knowing what to say.

A few minutes after Ally regains her composure, she says,

"Okay, the hotel has a menu for the restaurant a block away, and the food looks delicious. Let's check it out."

The girls are soon in "Crokante," where they are all sipping hot coffee laced with Irish liquor. They are talking about their family dynamics since Marisa left the girls after winning the Lottery and writing a bestselling novel.

Sarah says,

"Oh, I almost forgot. My mom said 'Hi' and for us to have a great time and be safe."

Janice says,

"That's so sweet. How is your Mom doing?"

Sarah smiles before answering,

"She's really good. My mom and sister can't wait for me to come back home now that she's running my boutique and she's a little flustered and tired."

Janice says,

"That's great. I actually just spoke to my mom. I'm supposed to take her on a vacation, so it will be nice to have quality time with her besides just having dinner together on Sundays. What about you, Melinda? Have you spoken to your family?"

Melinda says,

"Yeah, they're all good, can't wait to hear about our adventures and see some of our photos."

Janice says,

"Yeah, we're going to have some amazing photos to show our families. Ally, you spoke to your mom."

Ally is playing with her food, as she does not want to be transparent to the girls.

She looks at Janice, and then smiles before replying,

"She's great. I'm going to take her to the Aquarium when we get back. Now, can we eat? We have white water rafting in the morning, remember?

The girls continue to eat their main course, as the food is to die for. Sarah almost became ill, as she ate so much she barely made it back to the hotel. While a movie is playing with English subtitles, Ally has her notebook out, writing while everyone is watching the film and eating ice cream.

Everyone has something planned with their families. Moments like this are when I despise my mother. Although I know this is wrong, I even hate my sister.

She left me money and a note when she could have left me with her presence. It was always just her and me, she told me in a note.

I have so many questions that I want answered, but that will never happen.

Marisa did not give me her ear. She gave Janice the duty to tell me in a note.

I know she apologized, but still, does it really matter?

I'm still dealing with a druggie for a mother who uses Marisa as an excuse to be on the drugs.

The only thing I have planned is to take my mother to a clinic. I still can't locate my father, who I deserve answers from.

My life is an absolute mess, but I've continued to smile throughout this trip, while in actuality I'm crying myself to sleep every night, as everything that should hold value in my life actually means nothing.

No father, a druggie for a mother, and a dead sister: I have the best life anyone could ever ask for ☺

Ally

White Water Rafting

The girls are at Pacuare River, where they are listening to their instructor, Genesis, who seems to have a bad attitude as she gives some background information on the Pacuare River.

Genesis says,

"Alright, I'm only going to say this once, so listen or hurt yourself."

The girls don't like the way Genesis is lecturing them, and finally, Melinda whispers to Ally,

"I think we found the next person to prank."

Ally nods her head and continues to listen to Genesis talk about the Pacuare.

"The river is twelve miles long, and these are some rules you need to follow on your adventure. One: wear appropriate clothing. You ladies all have body suits, so we're good there. Wear sunscreen and sunglasses. Bring some wrapped snacks and water to drink while you're going down the river. Next, you should balance your boat; all riders should be strategically placed so that those of similar weight and paddling power are opposite each other. Please listen to this part, as this is very important: how to get unstuck from a rock. First, locate where the rock has caught the raft. Carefully shift the majority of the weight in the raft to the opposite side. Use your paddles to push against the current and rock, alright?

The last and most important step is staying safe. If you can, swim back to the raft. In the event you cannot get back to the raft, float on your back with your feet pointed down the river until you get to a shallow spot or to the bank of the river. Use your arms and paddle to guide you.

I hope you enjoy Pacuare River. Please remember, if you hurt yourselves, you signed a waiver and none of your money will be refundable."

The girls are now all dressed and very nervous. They take a few minutes and say a prayer before getting into the raft.

Melinda is the most nervous,

"Hold on. Let me say a prayer real quick."

Sarah says,

"Hurry up, Melinda."

"Don't rush me. Okay, please God keep me safe and if someone has to be hurt, let it be Sarah, as she made me rush this prayer. Amen."

Ally and Janice echo,

"Amen."

Sarah says,

"Really? That's how you feel?"

The girls all hop in the raft and start to push off the rocks to go down the twelve-mile river.

Ally and Sarah are very focused and have their eyes wide open as they move and shift their paddles to avoid the rocks.

Janice has one eye open and one eye closed. Melinda's eyes are shut completely, and she is simply dead weight in the raft, as she stopped paddling when the current became strong.

The girls finally make it through all the rough spots; the twists and turns of the river remind them of the winter Olympics and watching Alpine skiing.

The river is so wild, it makes them wonder why were they stupid enough to try something so dangerous. They are looking ahead, just salivating at the thought of being out of the river.

The girls are happy when they finally reach solid ground.

Melinda says,

"Thank God we're all alive. That river was amazing."

Ally looks at Melinda and says,

"How would you know? Your eyes were shut the whole time. If it wasn't for me, who knows if we'd be alive right now."

Melinda says,

"I disagree. I did some of the work, you know."

The girls are quiet and start to walk away from Melinda to indicate that they are not going to entertain her delusion that she was helpful when they were on the raft.

Melinda says,

"So you guys are just going to walk away? Alright, that's fine. Keep walking. I hope you guys have a good prank, because I'm not telling you my idea."

Ally screams back to Melinda,

"Of course we do. I'll tell you in the hotel."

Costa Rica Prank

The girls are in the hotel, ready to devise a prank for Genesis, as they found her tone extremely rude and cannot wait to teach her a lesson. Ally and the girls bounce around ideas for a prank that will deliver the punishment they will soon give Genesis.

Ally says,

"Okay, girls, what are we going to do?"

Janice replies,

"Not sure, but it needs to be good."

Melinda says,

"It needs to be better than good; it has to be epic."

Ally says,

"If you want epic, I know what we can do."

Janice says,

"There is nothing that can top Operation Pee Guards."

Ally says,

"Of all the people you talk to, I should be the one person you never doubt when it comes to a prank."

Sarah agrees with Ally.

"She has a point, Janice."

Janice says,

"Alright, so what is it?"

Ally says,

"We're going to do a sinkhole, then videotape it and put her on the net."

Janice asks,

"How are we going to pull that off?"

Ally tells them,

"Simple. We're going to break into Pacuare and camp out there, so we can see her fall in and catch it all on tape.

The prank is not as long as usual, but the expression on her face will be worth it? What do you guys think?"

Melinda takes a few seconds before answering,

"I think it's perfect to videotape it. She'll never be able to escape it."

Ally says,

"So, Melinda's in. What about you, Sarah?"

Sarah replies,

"Of course. Let's do it."

Janice is hesitant to say anything, but all the girls are staring at her waiting to hear her answer.

"Hmmmm. I guess we can break in and lose sleep to pull off this prank."

Melinda hugs Janice for agreeing to be a part of the prank.

Ally and the girls buy shovels and dress all in black. It takes them five hours to dig a hole big enough for Genesis to fall right in.

Now for the moment the girls have been waiting for. After working throughout the wee hours of the night, a few minutes before the park opens, Sarah puts a bit of dirt and leaves on the blanket so that it looks less suspicious.

The girls are now all spread out. Ally presses the record button on the camera and watches Genesis meet her fate. She is walking in with a cup of coffee and wearing sunglasses. Ally starts to count her steps to the hole.

She whispers,

"Ten, nine..."

...then zooms the camera in a bit more and continues to count Genesis' steps.

"...Eight, seven, six, five, four..."

Ally stops at three and continues to count on her fingers. As soon as she is left with just her index finger, they hear a colossal scream as Genesis falls into the hole, all of which they catch on tape. All the girls are laughing quietly, and run out of the park to find a cab. After walking a few minutes, they flag down a taxi to take them to the hotel so they can pack their stuff and get ready for Ireland.

While the girls are in the hotel, Ally takes the time to call her mom to see how she is doing, as today would have been a day when she would have gone over to check on her.

Ally calls and the phone just rings. She finds that odd, as she knows her mom has not left the house for anything because none of the stores are open.

Ally tries to call her mom again and she finally picks up.

"Hello, hello?"

Ally hears a sound of concern in her voice.

"Mom, are you okay?"

"Who is this?"

"It's your daughter."

"My daughter passed a few years ago. Are you playing a prank?"

"No, it's your other daughter, Ally."

"Oh, Ally. Sorry, honey, I had a rough morning." Ally hears her mom opening a bottle of prescription pills.

"Mom, what are you doing?"

"Nothing, I'm about to eat breakfast."

"Mom, no you're not. What are you doing?"

She giggles, and says,

"Ally, you know what I'm doing. Let's stop playing this game. My back is hurting, so I'm taking a pill."

"Mom, a pill is singular. What you're doing is taking *pills*; that's plural, and you're killing yourself."

"You can live without me. You proved that already, baby. You already found your way. You don't need me."

"Mom, yes I do. I need to finish packing, but I'll talk to you when I'm in Ireland."

"Alright, how long before you're back in the states?"

"About ten days. You're the first person I'm stopping to see. I love you."

"Love you, too."

Ally starts to cry on the phone. Her mom begins to slur her words and whisper to herself as she hangs up the phone.

Why My Mom?

*W*hy do I have to deal with my mom's selfishness? Although I do what I can for her, I don't know what else to do. As much as I want to help her, it will be a waste of money to send her to rehab. What she really wants is Marisa. I know she would love to have that closure. Hell, I want that closure from all of them.

I want the love of my sister, and I want to reconnect with my father and ask him why?

Why did he leave Marisa and me alone, knowing mom couldn't kick this habit?

I shouldn't have to worry about her. She doesn't even take the time to worry about herself. She wants to be numb to the pain of all the losses in her life. Who am I to make her change? Slowly, but surely, I too am changing and I know when I come back home I need to find my way.

I can't take care of her anymore. I need to take care of myself. I need to just deal with it when I get home, because I know I can't deal with it now.

I'm too far away and have so much pain in my heart when it comes to my mother.

Don't get me wrong. I love my mother, but I know I need to love me more. I can't deal with her addiction; she needs to deal with it. I can't make her clean; she has to want to be clean.

I now have friends whom my sister left behind so I can follow in their footsteps.

I'm grateful that Janice was such a wonderful guardian for those two years. She gave me my own bed, and there was always food on the table. I was in a group home before she came.

Janice is more my family then my own mother. I know that I need to just enjoy the positive people in my life, but it's hard when God births you in a bunch of chaos.

Ally

Ireland

T he girls are now in Dublin, Ireland, and are back on the same continent where their annual trip began. They just booked into the Westbury Hotel for the next four days. The hotel has so much to offer, as it has only top notch amenities. It is also close to some of the most historical places in Ireland.

Melinda says,

"Okay, you know I didn't want to be here. The only city in Ireland I've ever heard of is Dublin."

Janice tells her,

"There's actually a lot to see in Dublin. The places by the hotel have a lot of history and there's a lot going on."

Melinda says,

"I suppose I'll believe it when I see it."

Janice says,

"You're going to love Ireland: trust me."

Melinda asks,

"What are the names of these places?"

"The places we're going to visit are Trinity College, Iveagh Gardens, the little museum of Dublin, and Powers Court Town House.

Melinda says,

"Okay, I'm going to call it a night. I feel a bit jet-lagged from the flight."

All the girls say good night to Melinda and then they all go to bed as well.

Their Dublin adventure starts tomorrow, and they have to find a great prank to play on someone there.

Checking Out Dublin

The girls are up early to check out what Dublin has to offer. Their first stop is Trinity College. The girls have a short tour guide named Miles McCormick. Miles is a young man with an enthusiastic personality and a charming brogue.

"Hello," he says. "First and foremost, I want to say thank you for coming to visit this historical institution. Let me give you some background before we walk through the college, which was founded in 1592."

Janice is paying closer attention to what Miles has to say because she never went to college. She always loved learning, but just never felt that college was the best route for her, as she moved out of her house as soon as she turned eighteen, and did not feel she would be able to juggle school and work.

Janice asks Miles,

"So when the school was built in 1592, what was it like? Also, for the school to be open so long, how did they keep up with the funding for it?"

Miles tells her,

"That's a great question that requires a lengthy answer. Lets walk to the next area for all of you to view while I explain. Please follow me up the stairs."

Miles starts to answer Janice's questions while everyone follows him upstairs in two lines like students.

Miles explains,

"The first University of Dublin was referred to as the Medieval University of Dublin and is unrelated to the current university. It was created by the Pope in 1311, and for many years, consisted only of a Chancellor, lecturers, and students.

Although there is some debate about a new university at St. Patrick's Cathedral, following this, a small group of Dublin citizens obtained a charter in 1592 by way of Letters Patent from Queen Elizabeth, who incorporated Trinity College at the former site of All Hallows monastery, which is southeast of the city walls, and is provided by the Corporation of Dublin.

The first Provost of the College was the Archbishop of Dublin, Adam Loftus, and he was provided with two initial Fellows, James Hamilton and James Fullerton. Two years after it was founded, there were a few Fellows and students in this college.

Over the following fifty years, the community increased, and endowments, including considerable landed estates, were secured, new fellowships were founded, the books that formed the foundation of the great library were acquired, a curriculum was devised, and statutes were framed. The foundation Letters Patent were amended on a number of occasions by succeeding monarchs, such as by James I (1613) and, most notably, by Charles I (who established the Board—at that time the Provost and seven senior Fellows—and reduced the panel of Visitors in size) and were supplemented as late as the reign of Queen Victoria."

Miles then gives Janice a smile as he stops at the top of the stairs and leads them into the famous library. Miles gives some history of the Library of Trinity College, and tells them,

"This is the largest research library in Ireland. Because of its historic standing, Trinity College Library is a legal deposit library for the United Kingdom of Great Britain and Northern Ireland.

The College is therefore entitled legally to a copy of every book published in Great Britain and Ireland and consequently receives over 100,000 new items every year. The Library contains approximately five million books, including 30,000 current serials and significant collections of manuscripts, maps, and printed music. Three million books are held in the book depository, from which requests are retrieved twice daily.

The Library proper is composed of several library buildings. The original (Old) Library is Thomas Burgh's architectural masterpiece. A huge building, it originally towered over the university and city after its completion.

Even today, surrounded by similarly scaled buildings, it is imposing and dominates the view of the university from Nassau Street.

It was founded with the College and first endowed by James Ussher (1625–56), Archbishop of Armagh, who endowed his own valuable library, comprising several thousand printed books and manuscripts, to the College.

The Book of Kells is by far the Library's most famous book and is located in the Old Library, along with *The Book of Durrow*, *The Book of Howth*, and other ancient texts. The Old Library, which also incorporates the Long Room, is one of Ireland's biggest tourist attractions, and holds thousands of rare, and in many cases, very early volumes. In the 18th century, the college received the Brian Boru harp, which is one of the three surviving medieval Gaelic harps, and a national symbol of Ireland, which is now housed in the library.

The buildings referred to as the College's BLU (**B**erkeley **L**ecky **U**ssher) Arts library complex consist of the Berkeley Library in Fellow's Square, built in 1956, the Lecky Library, attached to the Arts building, and the James Ussher Library which opened officially in 2003, overlooks College Park, and houses the Glucksman Map Library. The Glucksman Library contains half a million printed maps, the largest collection of cartographic materials in Ireland. This includes the first Ordnance Surveys of Ireland, conducted in the early 19th century." At that point, Miles finally takes a breath.

The girls, along with the other tourists, start to roam around the rest of the library and continue to observe all of the different rooms there. That is, until Melinda has an idea for a prank.

She says,

"Hey, I think I have our new prank. Janice, Sarah, Ally, come here."

All of the girls walk over to Melinda to hear what she has to say.

"I think I know what our next prank should be. Oh yeah, what will work? That's it," she says to herself.

Sarah says,

"I don't like that look in your eyes. The last time we let you plan a prank, we almost went to jail, and were not in the states, so I really don't like that look in your eye."

Melinda asks innocently,

"What look?"

Sarah says,

"That look. You just did it again."

Janice says,

"Yup, I see what you're talking about, Sarah."

Melinda starts twitching and has a kamikaze smile on her face. Her eyes continue to twitch, which makes the girls take a step back.

Ally asks,

"So, what's your idea?"

Melinda replies,

"Well, I think we should borrow *The Book of Kells*."

Ally says,

"What? Really?"

Janice says,

"This girl really wants us to go to jail."

Melinda tells them,

"We won't go to jail. Let's go to the Iveagh Gardens and I'll tell you my idea in more detail."

Ally says,

"Alright, I guess listening to what you have to say won't hurt."

The girls are sitting at the Iveagh Gardens, which are very peaceful, and their beautiful, handcrafted marble sculptures, water fountains, and the energy there give a sense of tranquility. Melinda starts to debrief the girls on her prank.

"Okay, there are two ways for us to do this. We can steal the book in front of everyone, or we can break in during the night and take it."

Ally says,

"If we're really good at this prank, then we can do it in front of everyone."

Melinda says,

"I agree."

Ally asks,

"Okay, that's your idea: what's the plan?"

"Okay, I need you to distract the Librarian, then I need Sarah to distract the main security guard. Then from there, Janice and I will sneak the book off the shelves, but we need to remove the cover slip."

Ally asks,

"Why?"

"Because there has to be some form of tracking system, and I guarantee it will be on the cover of the book."

Ally says,

"This might actually work."

Melinda says sarcastically,

"Of course it's going to work. After all, I did come up with the idea."

Janice says,

"Don't be too confident, Melinda. We can go to jail, you know."

Melinda says,

"We'll do it tomorrow afternoon. Is that good?"

Sarah says,

"Good with me."

Janice says,

"I'm down."

Melinda says,

"Okay then, tomorrow it is."

The Book of Kells

It is the top of the morning and the girls are all groggy and still in their beds, except for Melinda, as she is excited to be point man or woman on this particular prank. She says,

"Girls, wake up, wake up."

Ally says,

"Give us fifteen minutes."

Melinda replies,

"Come on before I have to treat you all the way your moms used to when they woke you up for a school day."

Ally says out of the side of her mouth,

"Lucky for you, my mom never did," and puts her head back down on the pillow.

Melinda, tired of being patient, starts to go to all the girls and pulls the blankets off them, so the air conditioning will hit them and force them to get up.

She screams,

"You girls are forcing my hand. You leave me no choice. Next time, it's going to be ice water. Breakfast is in the living room. It's still hot; let's go."

After a few minutes of stretching and willing themselves out of bed, the girls are now in the living room, munching on breakfast while they're being debriefed by Melinda.

Ally says,

"So, tell us the details of this plan of yours."

Melinda replies,

"The plan is to distract two important players with beauty and a lot of questions."

Sarah says,

"Hey, before we go any deeper, what is so great about *The Book of Kells* again? And before you give me an attitude, Melinda, I'm sorry for asking, because I know we went there, but the gardens were so peaceful, it was hard to concentrate on your plans."

Melinda says,

"I would expect you not to pay any attention. Can someone please explain to Sarah what *The Book of Kells* is?"

Janice and Ally stay quiet, as they are in the same boat as Sarah. They also have no recollection of *The Book of Kells*. What was said in the museum went in one ear and out the other.

This causes Melinda to go off the deep end, and she starts to shake her head in disgust.

"How can you all not remember anything about the book? They have that book monitored with a security guard and cameras, but we can disable them easily. I just have to make a phone call to my cousin Tony. He loves hacking into things. He's all about trying to take down the system."

Janice says,

"Yeah, we're going to jail. I can see it now: 'Lottery winners go to jail on vacation'."

Melinda says,

"No, we're not."

Sarah says,

"It sure looks that way."

Melinda says,

"Whatever. Do me this solid. Go on the internet, Sarah, and read from Wikipedia what *The Book of Kells* is, please. How are we going to be enthused if we don't know what we're trying to pull off?"

Sarah pulls out her computer, clicks the link to Wikipedia, and searches *The Book of Kells*. Then she starts to read Aloud the page about the book.

The Book of Kells (Irish: Leabhar Cheanannais) (Dublin, Trinity College Library, MS A. I. (58), sometimes known as the Book of Columba) is an illuminated manuscript Gospel book in

Latin, containing the four Gospels of the New Testament together with various prefatory texts and tables. It was created in a Columban monastery in either Britain or Ireland, or indeed may have had contributions from various Columban institutions from both Britain and Ireland. It is believed to have been created ca. 800 AD. The text of the Gospels is largely drawn from the Vulgate, although it also includes several passages drawn from the earlier versions of the Bible, known as the Vetus Latina. It is a masterwork of Western calligraphy and represents the pinnacle of Insular illumination. It is also widely regarded as Ireland's finest national treasure.

The illustrations and ornamentation in The Book of Kells surpass that of other Insular Gospel books in extravagance and complexity. The decoration combines traditional Christian iconography with the ornate swirling motifs typical of Insular art. Figures of humans, animals, and mythical beasts, together with Celtic knots and interlacing patterns in vibrant colours, enliven the manuscript's pages. Many of these minor decorative elements are imbued with Christian symbolism, and so further emphasize the themes of the major illustrations.

The manuscript today comprises 340 folios and, since 1953, has been bound in four volumes. The leaves are on high-quality calf vellum, and the unprecedentedly elaborate ornamentation that covers them includes ten full-page illustrations and text pages that are vibrant with decorated initials and interlinear miniatures and mark the furthest extension of the anti-classical and energetic qualities of Insular art. The Insular majuscule script of the text itself appears to be the work of at least three different scribes. The lettering is in iron gall ink, and the colors used were derived from a wide range of substances, many of which were imports from distant lands.

The manuscript takes its name from the Abbey of Kells, which was its home for centuries. Today, it is on permanent display at Trinity College Library, Dublin. The Library usually displays two of the current four volumes at a time, one showing a major illustration and the other showing typical text pages, and the entire manuscript can be viewed on the Library's Digital Collections portal.

Sarah finally finishes reading and says,

"There, Melinda, are you happy? It is way too early to read all of that."

The girls walk out the door and head to the Library. When they get there, Melinda makes sure they know their final instructions so that the prank will be successful.

Melinda says,

"Ally, you just have to pull the Librarian away. I'll call Tony to take over their cameras for one minute and then Janice and I will sneak both the volumes into our book bags, and leave through different exits. We'll hang onto the book for the day. Once it breaks on the news, we'll find two students from the university and sneak it back on to campus with them. Everyone got it?"

The girls say in unison,

"Got it."

Melinda says,

"Alright, Operation Kells is a go."

Ally walks up to the Librarian and tries to introduce herself. The Librarian is staring at her computer screen.

Ally says,

"Hi."

The Librarian does not even say "hello" when Ally tries to introduce herself. Instead, she continues to stare at her computer screen.

Ally tries again.

"Hello?"

The Librarian finally looks up.

"Hello. I wanted to know if you can help me find a book?"

The Librarian says,

"I can, but if you go to the computer that is approximately thirty-five steps behind you, I'm sure you can find the book you're looking for."

Ally says,

"In all seriousness, I really wanted to let you know I'm in awe of you, as you make the stereotype of a Librarian fade away by how beautiful you are."

After she hears that, the Librarian begins to pay attention.

Ally now has her exactly where she wants her.

The Librarian takes off her glasses, removes her hair from its ponytail and says,

"You really think so?"

Ally replies,

"Of course. You don't see that guy looking at you?"

The Librarian tries to see the guy Ally is talking about, but Ally says,

"Wait, don't look. You don't want to chase him around the Library. Let's walk over there so he can get a good look at you."

"That would be nice, but I really need to stay right here."

"All we need is two minutes. All you have to do is grab those stack of books, and I'll do the talking to make the connection."

"Really? You think so?"

"I don't think so. I know so."

The Librarian tries to straighten her hair a bit and says,

"What the heck? Alright, let's go."

Now that Ally has done her job, she gives a thumbs-up to Melinda. When Melinda sees the signal, she scratches her forehead to signal Sarah to start her assignment. Sarah walks towards the security guard to take care of her part.

Sarah says to the chubby security guard,

"Hey, you."

The security guard looks back, as he thought she was talking to someone else.

Sarah says,

"Yes, I'm talking to you," at which point he starts to turn red. Sarah leans over to whisper in his ear. He smells her perfume for a moment, which leaves him paralyzed so that he can only listen to what Sarah has to say.

"I know you're busy, but can I just tell you that I love a man in a uniform?"

In disbelief, he asks,

"Really?"

"Really. What's your name?"

"Bob."

"Oh, Bob, I like that. Bob, I have a proposition for you. Do you care to listen?"

Bob tries to get back in security mode and says,

"What will that be?"

Sarah whispers in his ear,

"Let's go somewhere so we can talk. We're in a library, so I'm forced to whisper in your ear. What do you think? Do you think we can do that? Can we go somewhere so we can talk?"

Bob says,

"I can give you five minutes. I need to buy a cup of coffee. Would you like to accompany me?"

"I would love that. Let's go."

Sarah starts to walk away with Bob and signals to indicate she has completed her assignment.

Melinda now calls her cousin Tony, a computer hacker, to execute the third phase before she enters the area where *The Book of Kells* is kept.

Melinda says,

"Hey, Tony, you ready?"

Tony says,

"Yeah, I'm going to disable it in five seconds. They have a pretty good security system, so the best I can do since I'm not in the country is thirty seconds."

Melinda says,

"Thirty seconds? That's it? That's the best you can do for me?"

Tony answers,

"Yes, I'm sorry. I'm not allowing anybody to get hold of my IP address so they can track me. I'm counting down now, so I suggest you start walking."

"Alright."

Tony says,

"Okay. Five, four, three, two, one," and hangs up the phone.

Melinda and Janice start to walk towards *The Book of Kells*. As soon as they reach the room where the book is, Tony disables the cameras. Janice opens her book bag while Melinda scopes out the room, searching for the two volumes that are available for public viewing.

Melinda says to herself,

"Where is it? Where is it?"

Janice hisses,

"Hurry up."

"I'm trying."

"We have ten seconds."

"Found them, let's go."

Melinda pulls the volumes off the shelf as delicately as she can. As soon as she does, she puts them in Janice's knapsack and they walk out of the room.

Melinda and Janice walk calmly, heading for the doors, which should be easier to do with the Librarian away from her desk, and Bob the security guard away from his post.

This allows the girls to keep the books intact without having to remove any of the bar codes that might be on the book for security reasons.

Melinda and Janice move very calmly while Ally and Sarah start to disengage from their targets, as they know the assignment should be completed.

Ally asks the Librarian,

"Hey, did you get his number?"

"Yeah, I did, but are you sure he was looking at me?"

"Of course he was. You think I would just make that up? He did give you his number, after all."

"I felt as though I had to convince him?"

Ally did not know how to get out of the question just asked. She had slipped the guy a twenty without the Librarian knowing.

"No, that's not it. He was just a bit nervous; he's never seen someone as cute as you before."

The Librarian smiles and sits back at her desk and says to Ally,

"I guess you're right."

Ally smiles and says to the Librarian,

"Have a great day, and remember to smile at some of his jokes, even if they're not funny."

"Alright, I sure will. Thank you, Ally, for all your help."

"No problem."

Ally walks out of the Library and heads to the hotel, where the girls all agreed to meet after their assignments were completed.

Sarah is already outside of the library and is saying goodbye to Bob the security guard.

"Alright, Bob, thanks for the coffee. It was nice talking to you. Here's my number; call me sometime."

Sarah gives Bob a bogus number and walks back to the hotel. Bob is grinning from ear to ear, as his confidence is at an all-time high thanks to Sarah's interest.

Last Day in Dublin

The girls turn on the television in the wee hours of the morning and see the breaking news story.

The news anchor says solemnly,

"Breaking news in the city of Dublin as two volumes of *The Book of Kells* are stolen from the iconic Trinity College Library. There are no suspects at this time, but Dublin officials are taking this matter very seriously, as these books as a whole are valued at more than a million pounds.

After they hear those words, the girls wonder what they just got themselves into.

Janice says sarcastically,

"Thanks a lot, Melinda now we have the world looking for us."

Melinda says,

"So now it's all my fault? I can't believe you guys are putting the blame on me."

Janice says,

"Yeah, this is all your fault."

Ally butts in before a serious argument erupts between Melinda and Janice.

"Listen, we all played a part in getting us into this mess, and now we're going to get ourselves out of it. First things first: Melinda, you're going to call Tony and tell him that we need him to disable the cameras again, this time for three minutes, and not just the observation room, but the whole library, and especially by the Librarian's desk.

"Okay, I can do that."

Janice thinks and says,

"Why especially the Librarian's desk?"

Ally answers,

"Because Melinda, you're going to go and leave the books behind the desk, and Sarah, you're going to block the security guard's view. Do whatever you have to do—the more seductive, the better."

Sarah says,

"Got it."

Ally looks at Janice and says,

"You're running point. You're going to distract anyone who gets too close to Melinda when she's putting the books back. That alright with you?"

Janice says,

"I think I can do that."

"That's what I like to hear. Let's go and do this. The earlier we do it, the easier it will be for us to get in and out safely."

Melinda asks,

"What are we waiting for? Let's go. My hair and I cannot do jail time."

Ally and the girls rush out of the hotel to return what they have taken.

This has always been the plan, but the process is expedited by all the attention from the media.

The girls are now in the Library, where they start to undo their wrongs.

Sarah walks up to Bob and starts to flirt with him.

"Hey, Bob."

Bob, stuttering, says,

"Oh, hey, back again?"

As Sarah has Bob engaged instantly, he is no longer a threat to the mission at hand. Ally is now standing in front of the Librarian, getting ready to distract her, while Melinda has just finished talking with Tony on the phone, and he will disable the library cameras for three minutes.

Ally asks,

"Hey, did he call you?"

The Librarian says,

"Yeah, he actually did. He was so sweet."

The Librarian continues to talk Ally's ear off, while Melinda walks behind her slowly, opens up the book bag and place the books on top of a stack of others behind the Librarian. Melinda then walks slowly from behind the desk, where Ally is finding it hard to concentrate, as the Librarian blurts out all the things she likes about the man she met yesterday.

Ally sees that Melinda is clear and Janice did not have to distract anyone.

There are only three people at the Library, all of whom are sitting and reading. Ally and Sarah both break off their conversations and all of them are out the door before the cameras begin to work again.

A few minutes later, the Librarian turns around to pick up a new stack of books to organize the bookshelf, and sees volumes one and two of *The Book of Kells*.

Afraid of being accused of taking them, the Librarian simply slides the books on a random shelf and waits a few hours before calling the press.

The girls are packing for Japan and listening to the news, hoping to hear them talking about retrieving *The Book of Kells*.

"We have breaking news, as in a few moments, the head Librarian of Holy Trinity University will be holding a press conference. Here we go, she's at the podium to speak."

The news cuts directly to the press conference. The girls are all quiet, listening to the Librarian's words.

She stands in front of the Dublin press to speak.

"I am pleased to say that someone has had a change of heart. A few hours ago, I found both of the missing volumes of *The Book of Kells*. The University officials and I are just pleased to have these books back where they belong. We will look through our security system to see if there was a motive behind the initial theft. To confirm that these are the authentic copies, we will have several specialists from around the world verify their legitimacy."

Janice says,

"Thank God we're cleared. Let's get the hell out of here."

Sarah says,

"I hear you. I have our tickets for Japan."

Janice says,

"What are we waiting for? The sooner we get to Japan, the happier I'll be."

Melinda says,

"I'm ready when you are."

Ally offers,

"I'm ready. I'll go downstairs and catch us a cab."

The rest of the girls check the room to make sure all of their belongings will accompany them to their final destination: Japan.

Why Japan?

*W*hy Japan? Why do I have to go back? I wish I never picked this country out of the hat. Last time I was here, it was to say my final goodbye to my sister.

I don't have many memories, not because I don't want to, but I think it's a way to protect myself. My mind won't allow me to remember anything. I don't even really remember the moments with my sister that were supposed to be joyful.

In a way, I'm glad my memory is a little clouded. I don't know if I would be able to put a smile on my face if I didn't. I saw so much pain in my home and in the orphanage.

I did not commit any crime, but I still had to deal with everyone else's decisions that directly affected my life.

Going to Japan is like putting salt on an open wound, but I know this time I need to make ultimate peace with the situation with my sister and be at peace with myself.

Ally

Japan

The girls arrive in Japan, which is hard to deal with, as this was one of the four places they scattered Marisa's ashes. The girls book a suite in the Shangri-La Hotel, and drop their bags in the middle of the room, exhausted from traveling to the other side of the world. The girls instantly find a bed or a comfortable couch and go to bed, as they will be in Japan for the next four days.

The next morning, Janice is up early, drinking tea and looking at the view of Tokyo. Ally joins her with her own cup and they shoot the breeze before anyone else wakes up.

Ally says,

"Hey, what are you doing up?"

"Nothing, just taking a look at the city. It's so beautiful.

Ally says,

"Yeah, it's a wonderful city."

Janice turns a bland conversation into something more serious,

"Let me ask you something serious."

Ally says,

"Okay, what's up?"

"How do you really feel about being here?"

"Honestly?"

Janice puts her cup down, turns away from the window, and looks straight into Ally eyes.

"Yes, really? How you feel being here?"

"It sucks. I thought I was done grieving for my sister, but the truth is, I'm not. I really miss her. I miss her looking out for me. I wish we had these moments with one another, the ones that I have with you right now. I wish I had the same ones with her. All I can say is, it really sucks. I've had conversations with you that I wish I could have had with my sister. I'd be lying to myself if I said I want to be here."

Janice gives Ally a hug before saying anything, as she can only imagine how Ally feels.

"I hear you. We don't have to stay if you don't want too. We all understand."

"No, I need this. I really need to move forward. I love my sister, and I need to forgive her for not being here when I need her the most. I can't take care of my mom. It's becoming too hard, trying to take care of her and go to school."

"Yeah, I know, but I can tell you for a fact your sister would be very proud of you."

"You really think so, Janice?"

"Think so, no. I know so. Think about it. You forgave your mom enough that you try to provide stability in her life while you're in college."

"That's another thing my mom is not doing well at all. She continues to forget, and she still is very dependent on pills. She has no business taking those pills.

"I'll tell you what. Forget about us doing a prank. Let's cut the trip in half, do a bit of sightseeing, and pay our respects to your sister. Is that cool?"

"Yeah, that's fine, because I have a weird feeling that I need to hurry up and go home."

Janice smiles,

"Okay, it's settled then. Let's go see some places in the city and later on in the evening, we'll go to where we scattered the last bit of Marisa's ashes and pay our respects. Is that cool?"

Ally hugs Janice again and says,

"That is the best idea I've heard all day."

"Okay, I'm going to wake up Sarah and Melinda, and find a few things for us to do until the sun goes down, if that's okay."

Ally says,

"That will be perfect."

Checking Out Tokyo

T he girls plan to visit the Ancient Orient museum, but first they decide to check out some of Tokyo's famous buildings. The girls feel that from an architectural standpoint, Tokyo is the closest city that reminds them of New York.

The girls visit the Docomo building, Dentsu building, and the Tokyo Tower.

The Docomo building is the second largest clock tower in the world. The building broke ground in 1997 and was opened in 2000. The building is used largely to stock technical tools for NTT Docomo group. The greater portion of the building has colored lights. Solar energy is used in part to run the building. A compost separation system employed in the offices helps reduce waste and increase the recycling rate. Waste water is recycled, and rainwater is reused for the building's toilets.

Because the tower is not available for a tour, the girls just admire the building. While the view makes it understandable why people talk highly of this building, they are not as impressed because they are not allowed inside.

The second building is the Dentsu building, which was begun in 1999 and completed in 2002. It is the eleventh-tallest building in Tokyo, and was designed by French architect, Jean Nouvel. It was built over the first train station in Tokyo, and is located in the Hamarikyu Gardens. The Dentsu building is an excellent example of contemporary architecture.

The girls are mesmerized by the ceramic dots on the windows, which, in concert with computerized window shades, reduce expenditures for climate control. The Dentsu building has 70 elevators, including a special one reserved only for VIPs and executive management.

The outside is impressive, and the girls feel as if they are a hundred years in the future, as the inside of some parts of the building might be mistaken for a spaceship on *Star Trek*.

Ally says,

"Wow, this building is amazing."

Janice agrees and says,

"Yeah, it sure is."

Ally says,

"This building is so mind blowing. Here we are in a different country checking out these fancy buildings, when back home we have so many buildings that we never take the time to explore. Has that ever tripped you out a bit?"

Janice agrees,

"Yeah, you're absolutely right. We need to appreciate what's in front of us. Marisa even told us that. It's funny how she even wrote it down for us and we still don't do it."

Ally says,

"So true. Let's skip seeing this last building. I just want to go visit where we scattered Marisa's ashes."

Paying Respects

The girls go to the Tama River to pay their respects to Marisa. They are wearing white, as in Japanese culture, white represents the pureness of one's life or is worn to mourn someone's death.

Janice lights a small candle before talking about Marisa.

"I just want to say I love and miss you. I remember as kids we used to play silly games on our rooftop. We were so broke, we would play a game called 'My car.' We would claim every car that looked good.

We just shared so many memories that will never leave me. I guess what I'm trying to say is that I miss you and cannot wait to see you in paradise."

After talking, Janice puts her candle on a small wooden raft.

Sarah lights her candle next.

"When we met in college, I knew we were going to be great friends. You were just so welcoming and made me feel so comfortable.

I don't know if you knew it or not but you are the reason I didn't kill myself. These girls were writing nasty rumors and I couldn't live with myself until you came and simply asked me what was wrong.

Something told me to trust you and you never told a soul my secrets. You were a vault and kept it all in. I'm grateful to you because whether you know it or not, you gave me the proper perspective on my life. You allowed me to live. Thank you Marisa, thank you."

Sarah then lights her candle and puts it on the raft next to Janice'. Sarah starts to cry after putting her candle on the float, and Janice walks over to hug her while Melinda gets ready to say her piece.

Melinda smiles and wipes her eyes.

"Marisa, you were a lovely person. You always knew the right things to say and were the peacemaker. You gave me inner peace. Saying thank you does not do justice to all you have done for me, but thank you."

Melinda puts her candle on the raft and touches Alley on the shoulder.

Ally looks sad and says,

"Sis, I love you so much. You always protected me. You kept me out of harm's way always.

Every day, I go through the notebook that you left us to make sure I'm living the way you envisioned me to live, but I'm sending your notebook with this candle, as you have taught me well and now it is time for me to find my own way.

I will no longer allow your death to be a source of pain and anger, as your passing lets me know that there is a heaven and that I have another angel now watching over me. Love you, sis. See you on the other side."

Ally puts her candle on the raft as well as Marisa's notebook. She then says the Prayer of Jabez and pushes the raft out into the river. The girls take a moment to reflect on the raft floating into the river.

Janice asks Ally,

"How you feeling, kiddo?"

Ally says,

"I feel free of any ill will I had towards my sister."

Janice then asks,

"You ready to go back to New York?"

Ally takes a deep breath and says,

"Yes, let's go home."

Coming Home

The girls are at the Tokyo International Airport. waiting for the boarding announcement. Ally calls her mom to check in and see how she is doing.

Ally calls the house, but her mom does not answer. Ally tries again, but still gets no answer.

Ally asks herself, why is she not picking up. This is not like her. She always picks up, no matter what state of mind she's in. Let me try the cell phone I got her.

Ally starts pacing back and forth, hoping to get in touch with her mother, but still has no luck. She leaves a short voice message.

"Hey Mom, just wanted to see how you were holding up. There was a slight change in our plans. Call me, and if I don't pick up, please leave a voice mail. I want to hear from you and make sure that you're okay. Love you. I have to go, they're allowing us to board now."

Ally hangs up the cell phone and says,

"Please God, let her be okay."

The dispatcher radios to the pilot, *Good morning direct flight to NYC, JFK. Please approach the gate.*

The girls arrive in New York the following day. After the long flight, all the girls have jet lag and cannot wait to go to sleep. Although Ally is exhausted, she knows she needs to check with her mom, as she has yet to return her phone call.

Ally and Janice are outside about to get in a cab to go home.

Janice tells her,

"I can't wait to get in my own bed. Those hotels have nothing on my mattress. What about you? You've been up the whole time. You're going straight home, right?"

Frowning, Ally says,

"No, something is telling me to go uptown and check on my Mom."

Janice looks back at Ally in shock and says,

"At this time of night?"

"Yeah, something just doesn't feel right, you know?"

"I hear you, Ally. Let me go with you, just in case."

"You sure? You said you were tired."

"Yeah, I'm sure. I'd rather know that your mom is okay."

"Thanks, Janice. I don't know what I'd do without you."

Janice puts her arm around Ally.

"Stop it. You would be doing everything that you're doing. Now let's go see how your mom is doing."

Ally smiles,

"Okay, Harlem, here we come."

Ally and Janice climb in the cab and leave JFK. While in the cab, Ally keeps tapping her right foot.

"Why are you tapping your foot?" Janice asks in a concerned voice.

"Something just does not feel right. If I could explain, I would tell you exactly what it is, trust me."

"I know you would, but just don't beat yourself up before you know what's actually going on."

"I hear you. You're right. My mom just has been in a dark, dark place."

"What do you mean?"

"Let's just say that my mom tried to overdose a few days before our trip. I should have never left her. I would not be able to live with myself if I found something was wrong."

"I'm sorry. I wish you had told us. You know we could have chosen a different time to go on this trip."

"I needed this trip. I needed to get away. Sometimes the city can feel so suffocating."

"Janice says,

"That's why I moved to the suburbs."

"Looks like we're here. Driver, how much?"

The driver tells her,

"Forty-five."

Janice says,

"You know the ride is thirty-five dollars from JFK to here."

Janice digs into her pocket and hands the driver thirty-five dollars.

"Let's go, Ally."

As they hop out of the cab, Ally takes a deep breath before feeling around in her purse for the keys to open the door to the main entrance of her mother's building.

"Where are those damn keys? Okay, found them."

As they open the door, they smell an odor of breakfast being cooked, even though it is dinnertime.

"The elevator was not working last time I was here. I hope it works this time."

"Me too. I can't deal with trying to drag this suitcase up so many flights of stairs."

The girls are exhausted, and want to use the elevator, but after pressing the button, it never comes down.

Ally says,

"Damnit, this elevator never works."

Janice says,

"Let's take the stairs."

The girls shake their heads, annoyed that they have to climb five flights of stairs.

Ally and Janice finally make it to the door. Ally knocks. They hear smooth jazz coming out of the apartment.

Ally says,

"That's weird. My mom never has music playing."

Ally knocks on the door again, waiting for her Mom to open it, but to no avail.

"She still isn't answering."

Janice asks,

"You have a set of keys, right?"

"Yeah."

Ally uses her keys to open the door and screams for her mother, hoping for a response.

"Mom, Mom," she calls, but hears nothing, which makes her more nervous.

Ally rushes into the kitchen frantically, where she sees a bottle of pills with the cap on, filled, but not touched. Janice looks in the living room and does not see her. She then goes into the bathroom and screams.

"Mom, Mom! Why, why?"

Ally starts to cry. Janice runs to the bathroom to see what caused Ally's piercing scream.

Ally's mother is hanging from an extension cord attached to a metal pipe that sits directly under the ceiling. Written in lipstick on the mirror it says,

"I'm sorry. Check my sock drawer."

Ally and Janice leave the room, hysterical from what they've just seen.

Janice calls the cops, while Ally goes into her mother's bedroom and looks in the sock drawer to see what her mother has left.

Find Your Own Way

*T*o my baby Girl,

I'm sorry. I know this is selfish of me, but why should I live as your grown baby?

The only thing that was significant was giving birth to you and your sister. You do not need me, no matter what you think.

I've really been in a lot of emotional pain, and I don't even remember what I ate two hours ago. In case you don't know, I'm in the early stages of Alzheimer's.

When Marisa died, part of me died, and with me no longer having a sound mind, there's nothing for me to enjoy in this world.

I don't want you to continue to take care of me because of my depression, because of my sickness. So, I leave you to find your own way.

I had this information for you. It's a month old now, but there was never a proper time to tell you. Your father still lives in New York.

In my phone book, you'll find a sticky note with his contact information so you can reach him.

Just know your father loved you very much, but we had our issues. Please do not bear any ill will towards him.

Ally, I love you so much. Please continue to grow. You never needed me. You always found your own way.

You became my mom when I should have made a better effort to be yours.

Love, Mom

The Last Letters
Part Two

Goodbye

It is a cold winter day, and Ally is watching her mother being laid to rest, while Sarah, Melinda, and Janice stand next to her to offer moral support.

Father John says,

"Today we are here to pay our respects to a loving woman, Janice Santos. A God-fearing woman, she leaves behind her beautiful daughter, Ally. Before I lead us in the Lord's prayer, does anyone have anything they would like to say as we lay Mrs. Santos to rest?"

Ally says,

"I do. I wrote something down, so please bear with me.

"*Dear Mom,*

I know you were fighting too many inner demons. I just want you to know you will be missed. I will always do my best to remember the good times. For example, the day when we reunited and you cooked all of my favorite foods when I was a little girl. Or the times you saved your small amount of earnings to make sure Marisa and I could go to our weekly dance lessons and recitals. You made a lot of things possible. I'm sorry I was not there for you when you needed me the most, but that is my fault. I feel ashamed and disappointed in myself that I did not make a better attempt to make myself available.

You needed someone to let you know that you were loved. I failed you in that regard, and I have to live with that. Your lessons will be with me forever, both those you taught me directly and indirectly. I am forever in debt to you, as you gave me life.

Please tell Marisa I said 'Hi' and that I miss her, but at least she now has company I love you, mom.

Until we meet again,
Ally"

Ally avoids crying, but her voice is hoarse after she reads the letter to her mother.

Father John says,

"That was beautiful, Ally. Now let us bow our heads.

Our Father, which art in heaven,
Hallowed be thy Name.
Thy Kingdom come.
Thy will be done on earth,
As it is in heaven.
Give us this day our daily bread.
And forgive us our trespasses,
As we forgive those that trespass against us. And lead us not into temptation,
But deliver us from evil.
For thine is the kingdom,

> *The power, and the glory,*
> *For ever and ever.*
> *Amen"*

The father then takes dirt from the ground and gently makes a cross over the casket before walking away, leaving Ally and the girls watching as the casket is lowered into the ground.

Janice says,

"Hey, you want to hang out tonight? I don't have much going on if you want company."

Ally says,

"Yeah, I don't mind. We can watch a movie and order in."

Janice says,

"Sounds good to me."

Melinda asks,

"You mind if I come?"

Sarah chimes in,

"Me too."

Ally smiles and says,

"Of course I don't mind. You guys are the only family that I have left."

Pizza and a Movie

The girls are all at Ally's house, handing round the pizza that was just delivered.

"Who wants pepperoni?" Ally asks.

Janice replies,

"I want plain."

"Okay, what about you two?" she asks Sarah and Melinda.

Sarah says,

"I'll take pepperoni."

Melinda asks,

"Can I have both?"

"Sure."

Sarah says,

"If she's having both, I want both too."

Ally smiles and shakes her head, as she puts the girls' pizza on their plates.

Ally hands them around and says,

"Here you go."

Ally takes a seat and picks up the remote to look through Netflix to see what movies are on.

"What kind of movie do you guys feel like watching?" she asks.

Janice says,

"I feel like watching a drama."

Ally replies,

"I guess we can, but these movies have nothing on the drama in my life right now."

Sarah says,

"Don't say that; you're going to get through this. This is just a minor setback."

Ally sighs and does not say a word. She takes two deep breaths and walks into her bedroom. The girls look at her leaving the living room, unsure whether they should go with her and make an attempt to cheer her up.

Two minutes later, Ally walks back into the room with her mother's suicide letter in her hand.

Ally asks,

"Can I please read you guys the letter that my mother wrote?"

Melinda says,

"Only if you really want too. You just buried your mother. Are you sure you want to open up a new wound?"

"I want to read it because after I do, I would like you guys' opinion about what I should do."

Sarah says,

"If that's the case, then okay."

Janice says,

"Let's hear it."

Ally reads them the letter, and then asks,

"Well, I guess my question is, should I follow up on the lead that my mom gave me?"

Janice says,

"I think you should. I think it would be good for you to get closure."

Melinda says,

"I agree."

Ally says,

"Janice, do you mind going with me tomorrow to the address my mom left?"

Janice says,

"I don't mind. If she left a number, let's try and call first."

"Okay."

Sarah says,

"Let's change the subject. Let's pick a movie."

The girls agree and begin to watch *The Cold Lands*.

Phone Call

All of the girls spent the night at Ally's, leaving the television left on after the movie they were watching that night.

Ally gets up bright and early, while the rest of the girls are still sleeping. She stands with her cell phone in hand, pondering what to say.

Ally talks to herself aloud:

"Let's say I call him and he interrogates me. What do I say then?"

"Oh yeah, 'Hi, I'm the daughter you abandoned. Just want to take the time to reconnect, since I don't have a mother or sister anymore'."

Ally takes a deep breath and screams at the girls to wake up.

"Janice, Melinda, Sarah, wake up, wake up!"

Melinda, agitated by the way Ally is yelling to wake them up says,

"What, what do you want? You just ruined a great dream."

Ally says,

"I'm ready to make the call."

"If you're ready, than go for it, and let me go back to sleep."

Janice gets up, stretches, walks over to Ally in the kitchen, sits on a stool, and says,

"You've got this. The worst that can happen is that he refuses to be a part of your life. And if that's the case, he might be doing you a favor."

Ally says,

"You're right. Okay, here we go."

Ally picks up the sticky note and takes a breath after she has punched every number into her phone.

She looks at Janice, who smiles at her to ensure that she is doing the right thing.

Alley whispers,

"It's ringing, it's ringing."

"That's good."

Ring, ring, and then a woman picks up the phone.

"Hello?"

"Hi, I'm Ally. I'm looking for a James Santos."

The woman says,

"I'm sorry. I think you might have the wrong number. However, you're not the only one who asked for him, so maybe this number was his in the past."

A bit saddened, Ally says,

"Okay, thank you so much."

"No problem. Have a good day, and good luck trying to find him."

Janice says,

"That was quick. What happened?

"It's a dead end. She doesn't know who that is, but people do call that number from time to time. What are we going to do next?"

Janice says,

"I think what would be best for us to do from here is to look through all social media accounts, and white pages, and pull any photo albums that might have some writing on the back or additional information that can help us find your dad."

Ally says,

"That's not a bad idea. You sure Sarah and Melinda are going to be much help?"

Janice smiles and says,

"They will be when I wake them up and get them a cup of coffee."

Ally smiles, as she is always so amazed at how selfless Janice is.

"Alright, let me get the photo album that has pictures of him. Maybe it can help us find out where he lives."

Now all the girls are in the living room looking through all the potential resources that they have to find Ally's father.

Sarah is searching through the white pages, while Janice is browsing through social networks trying to find someone in New York with her father's name.

Ally and Melinda sit looking through photo albums, trying to find any clues that might have been left by Ally's mother.

Ally asks Sarah,

"Sarah, did you find anything?"

"I found a few numbers with your dad's name on them, but only three are in New York."

"What about you, Janice?"

Janice says,

"I got nothing."

Ally sighs,

"Same here. I've got nothing also, even with these photo albums."

Janice asks,

"What about your mother's apartment? You think there might be a clue there?"

I don't think so, and I'm not mentally prepared to go back into my mother's house yet. Hey Sarah, let me see those numbers. Maybe we'll find him that way."

Sarah walks over and hands Ally a notepad,

"Here you go."

Ally calls each number, but all of them have been disconnected. However, there were addresses to check for all of them.

Ally says,

"Okay. Well, the numbers don't check out, but there are addresses here. Maybe we can knock on these doors. Anybody want to come with?"

Janice and Melinda volunteer their services to check the apartments that were in the white pages.

Knock, Knock

Tomorrow I embark on a part of my life I did not want to know. My father has not been in my life since I was five. I was in bed when he spoke to Marisa, telling her,

"I'll be back. I'm going to the store."

This man has caused my sister and me so much grief. We waited for him for days, thinking he was coming back. We were so delusional. He didn't even pack and he lied. He really left us with what he had on his back, and smiled in Marisa's face, and waved to us before he walked out.

That's not a man, but a coward. I never received a birthday call or anything. He just never tried.

I have anger that is buried deep and it's now resurfacing. If he was in my life, more than likely even with my mother's illness, he could have taken me in. I'm sure that would have been an inconvenience for him, but Marisa and I would still have been together.

He is also the reason why I haven't trusted any man who has ever entered my life. Dan is one of the sweetest men I ever met, but I know I continuously push him away.

He always asks me why, and I'm writing all of this down, so I know I have an answer, I can tell him that the reason I'm not as open as I should be is because I haven't known a loving man since I was five years old. The family members I did have whom I knew did love me despite our issues are no longer here.

I truly have no family, but I want one so bad. I really want to be loved,

I truly want to be wanted. I lost my mother's side of the family simply because I do not know them, but I knew my mother.

I have a father, and from what I know, he's still alive, but I don't even know where he might live.

Three locations to check; I hope one of them is actually the James Santos I'm looking for.

Ally

The first location the girls check is the one closest to Alley's apartment on the Upper East Side.

Melinda, Janice, and Ally are all on the six train when this annoying dancer whom Janice and Alley grew up with starts clapping.

Alley and Janice put their heads down, hoping not to be noticed, and say to one another,

"Oh gosh, what are we going to do?"

Janice says to Ally,

"Just keep your head down. Maybe he won't realize it's us."

151

He's known in Ally's neighborhood as "Slim."

Slim is a tall, lanky, dirty looking kid with snot always running out of his nose. He is known around the neighborhood for trying to hit on every girl. He starts to clap his hands, and does a little hop before he breaks into his first dance step. He starts to break dance and almost hits people in the head. Before he can truly get into his dance, people are already complaining about him bumping into them, and everyone is pushing him away. Slim is not the best dancer.

After the debacle of him trying to dance on the train, Slim looks over and realizes that he knows Janice and Ally.

In an annoying voice, Slim asks,

"Janice, is that you? Hey, Janice, Janice, what's up, girl?"

Slim checks his face in the train window. He notices that he has a booger on the left side of his nose, and wipes it off with his right wrist.

Slim addresses her again,

"Janice, hey, boo, how are you? Haven't seen you on the block lately. What you been up to? Besides looking all cute and everything."

Janice says,

"You haven't seen me because I haven't lived there for a few years."

Slim says,

"Oh, alright, alright. Who's this? She reminds me of your best friend, what's-her-name. What's her name?"

Ally answers Slim before he can say anything else stupid.

"You mean Marisa."

Slim says,

"Yeah, that's it. Marisa, how are you? I know you want some of this Slim Jim."

Ally laughs, and says,

"Marisa is my sister."

Slim says,

"Wait, you're little Ally?"

"Not that little anymore. I guess this is our stop. Take care, Slim."

Janice says,

"Later, Slim."

"So, you just going to leave me like that? That's how you do? Okay, okay I like a little chase anyway. Janice, stop playing. I know you wanted me back in the day."

Janice and Alley step off the train without a word and are now walking to where Ally's father might be. Before Ally can walk to the elevator, the doorman asks her to go to the concierge's desk to check in.

The concierge says,

"Hello, how can I help you?"

Ally says,

"Hi, I'm looking for a James Santos."

"James Santos? I'm sorry. His name is not coming up. Let me try it again. Do you have an apartment number?"

"Yes I do: 5a."

The concierge smiles, and says,

"Okay, let me call the apartment and see if they have a James Santos residing there.

"Thank you."

The concierge picks up the phone to give the apartment a call. It rings once before an elderly woman picks up, and then the concierge asks,

"Hi, Mrs. Lee. Is there a Mr. James Santos who lives with you? I have a young lady here looking for him."

Mrs. Lee says,

"It depends. What is the young lady's name?"

The concierge whispers to her,

"What's your name?"

"It's Ally."

"Her name is Ally," he tells Mrs. Lee.

Mrs. Lee's eyes pop wide open.

"No. I don't know that name."

Before Ally can tell the concierge her last name, he hangs up the phone.

The concierge is startled that Mrs. Lee was so quick to get off the phone and says to Ally,

"I'm sorry. I don't think Mrs. Lee was being honest."

A bit disappointed, Ally smiles and thanks him, and walks out of the building with Janice by her side.

Janice asks,

"Ally, what are we going to do next?"

"Hop back on the train. Let's go check out the resident in the Bronx location. Brooklyn is too far out of the way."

"Okay."

Janice and Ally are back on the train uptown to the Bronx.

With the thirty-minute train ride ahead, Ally digs into her purse and pulls out her notebook to write down more of her thoughts.

I was hoping this would not turn out to be a scavenger hunt for someone who should want to be in my life. I did not realize how badly I really want to find him. Now I'm realizing I might need to know him at least for his medical background.

He obviously doesn't want me in his life, or else he would have come by to check on me. I hope I find him at this next place. I have questions that I want answered.

If not, life continues with my three friends and no one to call on Sundays. That's something I'm going to have to get used to.

Ally

The girls are now in the Bronx where they are about to knock on a door that belongs to a James Santos.

Ally takes a deep breath and walks up onto the porch to knock on the door.

A man's voice shouts,

"Who is it?"

Ally, a bit nervous, stutters so badly that she can barely say a word.

"It's Ally."

The man who might be her father opens the door and says,

"Can I help you?"

Ally, shaking a bit, pulls back her hair before answering him.

"Yes I'm looking for a James Santos."

"That's my name. How can I help you?"

Ally says,

"Sorry, I think I have the wrong James Santos. You see, I'm looking for my father and from the pictures that I have, I'm assuming you aren't him."

Ally than shows him a picture of her father when she was five years old.

The man smiles and says,

"You're right. That's not me. I wish I could be of more help, but I only have one child and he is nine years old. I hope you find him. Have a great day. Sorry."

"Thank you for your time, and sorry for any inconvenience I may have caused."

As the door closes, Ally walks back down the stairs.

Janice tells her,

"Hey Alley, don't look so down. There are other places we can check."

"Like where?"

"Like the orphanage."

"That's not a bad idea."

"We'll check tomorrow. Let's go home."

"Okay."

So today was a day that was no different from my everyday life. It had so many disappointing moments. I swear, I feel my life is being controlled by an evil little minion whose purpose is to make my day difficult.

I had no luck in finding my father today, and it is very disappointing knowing that I have nothing to show for my efforts. Another day without family, another day in this home alone.

I have everything that I thought meant something, but I am realizing I am nothing without my last name. I am a Santos. I am the daughter of Janet and James Santos. I lost my mother, but I know my father is somewhere. I know he resides in the city.

I just don't want to open up scabs that were on their way to healing, and are now wide open with acid being poured in the wounds. The orphanage gives me nightmares. The girls were mean and the counselors were meaner. The only one who actually wanted to be in the orphanage was Ms. Lopez. She always had a smile on her face.

Unfortunately, tomorrow I have to go back to a place I told myself I never wanted to go back to. This place carries so many scars compared to smiles.

Ally

The Group Home

Ally and Janice are standing in the lobby, waiting for the director of the group home so they can ask if there is anything in Ally's file that would help in her search for her father.

Ally has a flashback of what she saw growing up there. She remembers that, on one of the nights during her first week there, she was attacked and beaten up while she was sleeping. Each punch felt like a brick to her face and stomach, and each stomp or kick felt like God was throwing a boulder from the sky.

She opens up her eyes from the small flashback and finds that tears are flowing from her eyes, though she isn't making a sound. She is amazed how much she despises this place, as the only visit she received the whole time she was here was when Janice told her that Marisa had passed and that she was in the process of getting her out of the group home.

Mrs. Lopez walks out into the lobby to speak to Ally and Janice, but before doing so, she stops in the lobby, where she sees sodas on a table full of snacks. Mrs. Lopez grabs three sodas and a napkin full of cookies and walks over to Janice and Ally before speaking to her.

"Oh my God, Ally, is that you? How are you?"

Ally smiles,

"Hey. I'm doing okay."

"How can I help you? The girls who come here usually don't come back. What's up? You're not in trouble or anything, are you?"

"No, I'm not. I was hoping that maybe you have some information in my file that can be useful to me.

Mrs. Lopez looks a bit concerned. She straightens up and asks,

"Like what?"

Ally's voice starts to crack,

"Like my father. You see, my mother passed away and told me that my father still lives here in the city, and I just really need to know if I have any family. I refuse to believe that I don't. I have no sister and now I have no mother. They were the only two I knew were my family before my father left us. Please tell me that you can help me."

"I would love to help, but two years after someone leaves, we send our records to our state department. They should be able to tell you what's in your file. I can make a few calls so they know to expect you, if that's alright with you."

Ally is disappointed that the file is not where she expected it to be, but she smiles and says,

"Alright, I would appreciate that."

Ally shakes Mrs. Lopez' hand before walking out."

Janice asks Ally,

"What do you want to do now?"

"I want to go home and get some Chinese food and sit home alone by myself."

"That's fine, but just remember that Sarah, Melinda, and I love you. I know we're not your blood, but we all care about you very much, and I know we're going to find your dad. Just have faith on this journey, alright?"

Ally hugs Janice after those words, and hails herself a cab to go home. Janice walks two blocks down to the bus stop to return to her condo.

All Alone

Ally is all alone on the couch eating Chinese food and reading a letter that Marisa wrote to form a connection with her sister. Marisa's letter says "28 Days":

Do I tell my friends I have a month to live? Do I tell my friends that I won the lottery? What is a month? Is that thirty-one days or exactly four weeks? Do I tell my mother, whom I haven't spoken to since I was eighteen? I let three years go by; was it all worth it? Not talking to her because she had a problem that I could not fix? I don't know how I should feel. Should I be joyful or deeply saddened that I don't care? I love my sister, and I lost her because my mother could not kick a bad habit.

Do I pray to God to give me another miracle? Maybe this time, it won't be for abundance. I would exchange that dream for a clean bill of health. I have twenty-eight days, and I guess all that is left is to live life with no limits and no more regrets.

Marisa

Ally is in a very somber mood, as she just wants a form of connection to her ancestry.

Ally picks up the phone to listen to her mother's voice mail.

Janet's voice sounds as delighted as if this was the only phone she ever owned. Her voice is so elegant.

"Hello, this is Janet. I am not able to come to the phone. Please leave a name and number and I will be sure to give you a call back."

Ally has a big smile on her face and then she opens her laptop to look at footage of her father reading a story to her and Marisa.

Looking at the footage, she starts to tell herself,

I need to find my father. It makes no sense for me to reconnect if he wants nothing to do with me, but I have to see for myself. When I go to the Municipal building tomorrow, I hope there is a clue to find him."

The Real James Santos

Mrs. Lee hears a knock at the door of her apartment and says,

"Who is it?"

A man says,

"Me."

Mrs. Lee says,

"Me who?"

"Your son."

Mrs. Lee smiles and opens the door and there is James Santos and his three children: James Junior, Jose, and Mallory.

As they all walk into the apartment, Mrs. Lee says to James,

"I need to speak to you."

"Mom, can we speak at dinner? We just got here."

"No, I need to speak to you now."

James, seeing that she really wants to talk to him, walks to the back and into his mother's room. Mrs. Lee follows him into the room and closes the door before she speaks.

She says,

"So, a few days ago a girl came asking for you."

James looks puzzled.

"Who would that be? Nobody should be asking about me."

"Not even your daughter?"

"What? She called? You didn't tell me. I have been trying to reach my girls for years."

Mrs. Lee says,

"Don't worry about it. You should not be worried about those girls. Look what you made of yourself."

"Those are your granddaughters. Why didn't you tell me? I can't have this conversation with you. Now that I know they're looking for me, you should know that I will be trying to find them. I wrote so many letters to their mother, but she never gave them even one letter that I wrote."

His mother starts to say something mean-spirited, but before she can say anything, he opens the door and says,

"Kids, let's go. Grandma is not feeling well. I'm going to make you guys a plate and we'll eat it at home."

James Santo is now home, where he reads the first letter that he wrote to both his daughters.

Dear Marisa and Ally,

I know it's been some time since we spoke. I just want to let you know that I love you both and it was not easy for daddy to go away. Your mother and I were not getting along. To make sure my beautiful girls stayed happy, I needed to leave.

Leaving had nothing to do with you girls. Daddy just made a big mistake that made your mother mad at me, and she had every right to be so.

Marisa, I hope you are having a good time in your dance class. Ally, I hope you're eating all your vegetables. They will make you the smartest and strongest girl in the world.

Marisa, continue to do well in school. Remember, hard work will always prevail.

To my daughters, you are my world. I love you both, and hope to get a letter soon. I love you more than I could ever show.

Love, Daddy

James puts the letter away in a locked box in his closet. When he hears his wife Robin's footsteps approaching the bedroom, he rushes back to the bed while she enters and says,

"Hey."

James smiles and says,

"Hey sweetie, how was your afternoon?"

"Nothing much. How was your Mom?"

James says,

"It was okay. My mother and I got into a bit of an argument."

"Really? What did you argue about?"

James smiles and says,

"Nothing, really. You know how we can get from time to time."

Robin smiles and says,

"It must be something major if you made all the kids a plate to go. I really would like to know."

James' mood changes as he tells Robin,

"It's not something I'm ready to share with you."

Robin says,

"We've been married for twelve years and together for fourteen. You're really not going to tell me?"

James kisses Robin on the forehead, and says,

"I'm going to bed," and turns off the lamp on his side.

Robin is upset, and turns to her side of the bed and tries to get comfortable before going to sleep.

"This is not over James. I'm going to find out what the hell is going on, either by you telling me, or me looking for the answer. The decision will be yours."

James keeps quiet for a few seconds, making sure he has nothing else to say, and then says goodnight again.

Another day looking for Santos.

Ally has all the girls wait for her in the lobby, as she is in the Municipal building being helped by a young woman named Monica.

Monica asks Ally,

"Can I have your last name then first name, please?"

Ally says nervously,

"Santos, Ally."

Monica types her name in the database and after doing so, smiles and says,

"I actually have your file out already. Ms. Lopez told me that you were going to come by. May I ask the reason why?"

"I was hoping there was something in my file that will help lead me to my father, like an address or a phone number, and maybe the reason why he couldn't become my guardian."

Monica smiles, takes a key chain that is on her wrist, and opens up her file cabinet. She slides Ally her file, and starts to talk about it while Ally opens the file.

Monica says,

"The file does not have much about your father, as he wrote a letter to your mother giving her full custody of you and your sister. The rest of the information on that paper is all medical information on both your parents; but I am not at liberty to look for anyone else's file other than your own."

Ally is upset and thinks, so my father never wanted me, but I'm stupid enough to go looking for him. This was a bad idea.

Monica allows Ally to read the letter that her father wrote to her mother who brought this letter in as proof to the court when Marisa was seeking to be emancipated.

I, James Santos, give my parental legal rights to my daughters, Marisa Santos and Ally Santos, to Ms. Janet Ogden. If anything is to happen to her, please allow my children to live with one of Ms. Ogden's family members, or my mother, Mrs. Leslie Lee.

The reason I'm signing over my rights is because I am not in a position financially to support them and will be leaving the country and am not sure of the date of my return.

James Santos

Monica says,

"That letter is the only thing that has your father's name on it. I'm sorry."

A bit puzzled and still looking at the letter, Ally asks Monica,

"Do you mind if I make a photocopy of the letter?"

Monica smiles and says,

"No I don't, but if anybody asks you where you got the letter, you did not get it from me."

Ally smiles and says,

"Of course not."

Ally takes the letter and heads out of the office and into the lobby where the girls are waiting for her.

Sarah asks,

"How did it go?"

"Not as well as I wanted, but I think I have a stronger lead now."

Melinda, curious to know what Ally means, asks,

"How so?"

"Remember the concierge who called that Mrs. Lee?"

Janice thinks for a bit before answering,

"Oh yeah, that's the lady who asked for your name, and after the concierge told her, the lady said 'no' and hung up, right?"

Ally looks at Janice,

"That's my dad's mother."

Sarah, slow to make the connection to who that is to Ally, says,

"So wait, does that mean Mrs. Lee is your grandmother?"

Melinda gives her a light smack on her blond head and says to Sarah,

"You know, sometime it amazes me you made it this far in life. It really does."

Janice intervenes before an argument starts between the two.

"You guys are embarrassing. Let's leave, and tomorrow we'll speak to the concierge again to see if he can give us more information on Mrs. Lee, since she obviously lied about knowing Ally's father."

Ally says,

"That sounds good, but I'm going to need to do this on my own. I don't need anybody else to help me."

Janice asks,

"You sure you don't want any of us to come with you?"

"Yeah, I'm sure. I need to know why my grandmother turned me away."

Early the next morning, Ally is eating breakfast just across the street from her grandmother's apartment. To calm herself down, she pulls out her notebook to write a letter to her grandmother. She wants to say what she feels now, just in case her grandmother chooses not to listen to her. At least she can leave the letter with the concierge.

Dear Leslie Lee,

You might have heard of me, or maybe you haven't. In case you haven't, I am James Santos' daughter, Ally. The reason why I am reaching out to you is because I no longer have any family. My mother and sister died and I would really like to connect with my father. He is the only family member that I know of. That is, of course, until I found your apartment with my father's name in the white pages.

I do not remember much, but from the photos I have of him, I can tell he loved me as well as my older sister, Marisa. He was a very loving man.

I have a lot of questions that only my father can answer, so please let him see this letter so he knows I am looking for him. Thank you. I will come here every Sunday for the next month until you answer me or he does. Have a great day,

Your granddaughter,
Ally

After writing the letter, Ally smiles and puts her notebook back into her purse. She takes a deep breath before walking across the street to speak to the concierge again.

"Excuse me, sir. I wondered if Mrs. Lee was home?"

The concierge smiles,

"You don't have to call me sir. Alex will be just fine."

Ally smiles and says,

"Okay, Alex, can you please see if Mrs. Lee is home?"

179

"Sorry, I can't. She told me specifically not to call her if you came here asking for her."

Ally, not sure what to say to Alex, feels this is her only opportunity to find her father. She says,

"What if I do something for you if you do something for me?"

Intrigued, Alex asks,

"What could you do for me that I can't do for myself?"

Ally puts herself in a jam, but goes for it anyway and says,

"I'll cook you something delicious."

Alex looks into her eyes and then puts a note pad in front of her and says,

"Write your number here, please."

She grabs the pen and looks him right in the eyes as well, and without even looking down, she writes her number on the pad, gives him a seductive grin, and says,

"Make the call."

Alex picks up the phone and calls Mrs. Lee, waiting to hear someone pick up, but once again, there is no answer.

Alex says,

"I'm sorry, Ally, nobody picked up, but I hope you will still honor your part of the deal."

Ally then rips the page out of her spiral notebook, hands him the letter she wrote across the street in the diner, and says,

"Of course I will. Just give this to her and if she reads this in front of you, please tell me what she says."

"Alright, I will."

Ally walks away and says with her back turned to Alex,

"Meet me tonight. I'll text you my address."

A few hours later, Alex is on high alert, waiting to spot Mrs. Lee. Ten minutes before he is supposed to clock out, Mrs. Lee walks into the building and Alex stops her.

"Excuse me, Mrs. Lee. May I talk to you for a moment, please?"

Mrs. Lee replies,

"Sure Alex, what do you need, honey?"

"A young woman asked me to give this to you. She didn't mention her name, just said that it was important that you read it."

Mrs. Lee, not believing anything he is saying, says,

"Alex, everyone who lives in this building pays you good money to get simple information. For example, name and number, and just in case they seem a bit suspicious, sometimes you can even ask for I.D. I suggest you start doing that before I speak to the powers that be."

Alex, nervous about losing his job, answers,

"Yes, ma'am, I will," and hands Mrs. Lee the letter Ally wrote.

Mrs. Lee heads to her apartment and once inside, she hangs up her coat and purse before sitting down in front of the coffee table to read the letter Alex gave her.

After reading the letter, and realizing it is from Ally, she calls James' cell phone to tell him about the letter, but changes her mind, burns the letter instead, and tells him to come over for dinner, as she wants to discuss some properties she owns and welcomes his opinion.

Four People, Two Dinners

Ally is listening to Frank Sinatra while prepping dinner before Alex comes over. While she's cooking, Sarah calls Ally.

"Hello?"

Sarah says,

"It's Sarah. I'm not doing much, and I'm bored. What are you up to?"

Ally smiles and says,

"Making dinner."

Sarah screams through the phone,

"You can barely cook!!! What are you making?"

I think I'm going to make baked chicken and a salad: something simple."

Sarah asks,

"And that's all for you?"

Ally smiles and says,

"Not really. I'm actually making dinner for me and that concierge guy."

Sarah laughs,

"Really? His name is Alex. Janice told me about him. I didn't know you were into him."

Ally smiles, and says,

"He did me a favor and gave my grandmother a letter I wrote, so I'm just showing my appreciation."

"That's nice of you. If I was you, I would have ordered the food, since you can't cook for shit yourself."

Ally hears a knock at the door. She puts the chicken in the oven and cuts short the conversation with Sarah.

"I have to go, Sarah. I hear a knock at my door. I think its Alex."

Across town, James and his mother are eating dinner at opposite ends of the table. They do not speak until James asks,

"What do you want, Mother?"

"Your daughter came by today. I believe her name is Ally."

"Okay, so what did she say?"

"I didn't see her. She wrote me a letter and the concierge gave it to me."

James is excited,

"Where is the letter?"

"It's in the fire place."

James voice becomes hard.

"What do you mean it's in the fire place?"

"I mean I burned it. Why do you want to ruin your life? The best thing you did was cheat on that girl. She kicked you out of your house, and that's when your life changed for the better. I did you a favor. Consider it a blessing."

James replies angrily,

"What is wrong with you? This is my daughter, and not a day goes by that I don't regret what I did to my baby girls."

"Well, it was Ally. She mentioned your other daughter, Marisa, but said she would be here sometime next week or something like that. Be happy I told you that much, and eat your vegetables; they're getting cold."

James drinks the rest of his wine, takes the napkin from his lap, wipes his mouth, walks over to his mom, kisses her on the forehead, and says,

"You need help. Good night, mom."

James picks up his coat from the coat stand and walks straight out the door.

Mrs. Lee calls to James as he is walking out of her apartment,

"I love you too, James."

Back at Ally's house, she and Alex engage in a lot of small talk while they are eating dinner, until Alex brings up who he gave the letter too.

"Hey, I just wanted to tell you that I gave the letter to Mrs. Lee."

Ally's eyes widen as Alex changes the subject, and says,

"Did she read it in front of you?"

Alex shakes his head as he chews his food, and after he swallows, says,

"But she gave me a stern talking to."

"Really, like how?"

"Just reminding me of my job description, how I need to check people's IDs if I want to keep my job.. Sorry to be so nosy, but why is her getting that letter so important?"

Ally smiles, and takes a sip of her wine before answering Alex' question.

"I'm not going to answer your question now, but I'll give you the answer on our next date.

Alex also smiles and says,

"If that's the case, I'm going to end this night early."

Ally is confused.

"Why is that?"

Alex flashes his charming smile and says,

"So we can move on to our second date. Thanks for dinner, and have a good night, Ally."

Ally walks Alex to the door, and tells him,

"Have a good night, Alex."

"I hope you do the same."

Secret Letters

*H*e is amazingly handsome and tall. I wonder if this is what my sister envisioned when she wrote about a man. Alex' hands feel strong, but still soft as cotton.

His smile is so charming and his voice just calms me down. At moments like this, I wish I had my sister so we could talk about boys and I could get advice from her. I even wish my Mother could tell me the things I should look for in my life as well.

He has these soulful eyes, where I can tell everything he is saying to me is the truth. That is so hard to find, but he just has such warmth to him. I am so truly appreciative he gave that letter to my grandmother. I just hope something comes of it, because finding my father is my mission, although Alex would be a bonus. Progress was made tonight in both respects, and for that reason alone, I am very grateful.

Ally

James is home and tired from the mentally fatiguing day with his mother. He is drunk and reading a copy of the second letter he wrote to his daughters.

Dear Marisa and Ally,

I hope all is well in school. I just know you ladies are doing phenomenal in school, and want to let you know I am proud of you, and that you will always be daddy's little girls.

Remember the prayer that your grandmother always told you both to say whenever she would babysit you two.

I say that prayer every night and I can't help but think of my babies.

"*Oh, that you would bless me and enlarge my territory! Let your hand be with me, and keep me from harm so that I will be free from pain.*"

I can't help but miss my babies. I love you so much and more than I could ever show.

Love you always,
Daddy

Walking In

James has a big smile on his face as he picks up another letter to read. While he is doing so, his wife walks into the room.

She stands over him while he is reading the letter, but before saying anything, she grabs the black lock box to see what has been in there all those years.

"Robin, give that back to me."

"No, why are you keeping secrets from me?"

James tells her in an aggravated tone,

"Give it back to me now or else."

"Or else what?"

Robin opens up the box, and sees the bunch of letters. Before reading any of them, she assumes the worst.

"What the hell is this? You're writing letters to some bitch. Are you not happy with me?"

James gets up off the bed, walks towards her and holds onto her wrist while talking to her. He has never put his hands on a woman in that way before, and says to Robin,

"If you call my daughters bitches ever again in your life, I'll make sure of a divorce and I will make you go through so much legal trouble that anybody who would take the time to represent you would be an absolute fool. Now you can read the letter that you were about to rip up, bitch."

Robin's mouth is hanging open she is so taken aback at the way James just spoke to her, as he has never spoken to her like that in his life.

She reads the letter out loud.

To my loving daughters, Marisa and Ally,

I am sorry I was not around for your birthday party. I hope this letter brings you both joy, as daddy misses you two so much. I cannot wait to see you guys. I am still doing my best to make your mother happy so she will allow me to see you two. Please continue to do well in school. Do not forget to say your prayers, and no matter what life throws your way, remember to stay positive. I love you both forever and ever.

Love, Daddy

"What the hell, James. How come you never told me you had a daughter, excuse me, two daughters?"

James says,

"Go to bed, Robin."

Robin jumps on top of him, grabs him by the shirt and yells,

"How come you never told me you had a child by another woman?"

James looks Robin straight in the eyes and says,

"Because you are the other woman."

James then pushes her off him with one arm and walks towards the living room, where there is a bar filled with Johnny Walker black, and a glass.

Robin follows him, still asking him questions.

"James, how old are your daughters? And did you cheat on me?"

James drinks the glass he just poured, and then proceeds to drink from the bottle.

"I did not cheat on you. I cheated on my ex, who was their mother. We were having our troubles. She became addicted to drugs and I mentally checked out of the relationship a long time ago. The reason why the relationship between me and their mother ended is because you became pregnant, and I finally had the balls to tell her. She told me to leave and all I did was pen letters to my children, hoping for a response, but I never received one."

Robin is sad that she broke up a family and created her own, although she did not know this all took place fourteen years ago.

She says,

"Okay we need to find your daughters. How do we start?"

James says,

"My mother is the only one who has had contact with one of them."

Robin says,

"The only reason she was being so difficult was because she thought you wouldn't tell me that you had two children before we had our three. Although those words never came out of her mouth, I know that's the reason why."

"If you feel that's the reason why, do you think we can go over to my Mom's next weekend to talk to her?"

Robin says,

"You know what, honey, let me go over there by myself and I'll ask her to give me the details."

Shocked, James asks,

"You would really do that for me?"

Robin smiles, walks over to him, and kisses him on the lips before saying,

"Of course I would. I see how important this is to you."

James looks her in the eyes and says,

"This is why I love you. Thank you."

Robin walks out the room and says,

"Love you more."

No Church on a Sunday

Robin walks into Mrs. Lee's home to continue the conversation she had with her husband.

"Hey, Mom, how's your week been going?"

Mrs. Lee digs into her purse for a cigarette, taps the bottom of it before she puts it in her mouth, and says,

"What the hell are you doing here, Robin?"

"We need to talk about this daughter of his who keeps harassing you, so do me a favor."

Mrs. Lee takes a puff,

"How do you expect me to do that? I burned the letter."

"However, you did receive a call from the concierge maybe he can get in contact with her if possible, so bring her up to your home and I can take care of this."

"How am I supposed to do that? You know I can't miss church."

"Do you want to keep the money in the family that we know exists? You know James has cancer and has been feeling really ill. We can bribe this girl to make sure there is no dispute over his estate. He has yet to write his will, and you know how sensitive he can be, so it's best if we find a way to leave him out of the situation, wouldn't you agree?"

Mrs. Lee taps her ashes into the ashtray and says,

"Alright, no church, I guess."

Robin smiles and says,

"Make the call to whoever you need to."

Mrs. Lee calls Alex.

"Hello?"

Mrs. Lee says,

"Hey Alex, I read the letter that lady dropped off. If you see her, can you tell her to come up?"

Alex is shocked by her words, but says,

"Oh, okay, no problem, Mrs. Lee. I'll be sure to do that."

Alex then calls Ally to give her the news. The phone rings three times and then he hears Ally's voice mail, and leaves a short message.

"Hey, Ally. It's Alex. When you get this message, call me back as soon as possible. Bye."

As soon as he hangs up his cell, Ally walks through the door and comes over to him.

She says,

"Hey, what's up, Alex? How are you?"

"I'm good. Did you get my message?"

"No I just got off the train. Can I wait here for an hour or so? I was hoping to catch Mrs. Lee."

"That's actually the reason I called you. She wants you to go up to her apartment. I'm going to call her and verify that. I hope you don't mind. It should only take a minute."

Ally says happily,

"Why are you asking me? Hurry up."

Alex receives confirmation that Ally is requested to go upstairs to see Mrs. Lee.

Ally rides the elevator up to the penthouse floor. The ride feels like it is taking forever and Ally remembers the prayer her grandmother taught her and Marisa when they were little.

"Oh lord, that you would bless me indeed, and enlarge my territory, and that your hand will be with me that you will keep me from evil and that I may not cause any pain."

Before she can say "Amen," she reaches her floor and the door opens.

Ally takes a deep breath and knocks on the door twice. Instead of Mrs. Lee opening the door, a woman she doesn't know answers it.

Ally, who expects the older woman, stutters on her first word,

"Hi, are you Mrs. Lee?" Ally asks Robin.

"No, I'm your father's wife. Come in, please, and have a seat."

Ally, not liking her tone, walks in cautiously, sensing that the invitation to the apartment was more of a trap.

Once she's in the living room, she takes a comfortable seat while Robin speaks.

Robin is wearing an all-black dress. She opens her purse and pulls out an envelope filled with cash. She slides it over to Ally, and says,

"Don't come back here looking for my husband. There's nothing in that envelope but hundreds. You don't need him. He left you, your mother, and your sister. Which one are you again? Ally or Marisa? Either way, it doesn't really matter. I caught him reading some letters that he wrote you."

Ally, who has never heard about any letters, is confused and hurt by the venom in Robin's words.

"What the hell are you talking about? I don't know of any letters he ever sent me. That man abandoned me, but he's the only family I have, and that's why I'm trying to reach out to him."

Robin gives her an evil grin, and says,

"Take the money and leave. Don't try to reach me or Mrs. Lee. We want nothing to do with you, especially my husband."

Ally says,

"So how come he can't tell me that for himself?"

Mrs. Lee comes in from the back room. She has heard their whole conversation, and decides to put in her two cents' worth.

"It's real simple, darling. Your mother was a mistake, and you and your sister were even bigger mistakes.

Ally refuses to take any more disrespect, and slaps Robin hard across the face. Robin falls head first into the coffee table, breaking the glass.

Ally then looks at her grandmother, who is in shock at what happened to her daughter-in-law. Ally says,

"You're next," and then walks out of the elaborate penthouse.

The elevator doors open to the lobby and Ally is so angry she heads straight to the door. Alex sees her face, and asks,

"Ally, you okay?"

Worried she might take her anger out on him, she walks to the door, and without looking in his direction, says,

"I'll text you."

James is in his house watching the children when he sees his wife walking in the door, and sees that her right eye is swollen.

"Robin what the hell happened to you? Who did this to you?"

Robin says,

"Nobody."

"Don't lie to me. Did my mother do this to you?"

Robin opens the fridge and takes out a bag of frozen broccoli,

"No."

James asks,

"Then who?"

Robin, not wanting to lie to her husband, says,

"Your daughter smacked me, that's who."

James looks his wife in the face.

"What did you do to her that made her hit you?"

"What makes you think I did anything to make her want to hurt me?"

"Because I actually know my wife, and I know you have a tendency to say things that are totally rude and off the wall. So please tell me."

"I tried to give her money and told her to leave my family alone, okay? That's the damn truth. I said something about her sister and her mother, and she got up and smacked me."

James gets up, grabs his coat, puts on his hat, walks over to his wife, and tells Robin,

"I'm happy she smacked you on the face, because I'm going to smack you where it really hurts. I suggest you lawyer up."

Shocked, Robin screams while James is walking out the door.

"What does that mean, James? James, James, come back here. Baby, let's talk about this. James? Let's talk about this."

After he leaves, Robin makes a cocktail and sits in the living room, realizing she is now paying for an awful mistake. What once seemed like a great idea now looks like a plan that is soon to destroy her marriage.

Ally is still very angry about what happened earlier in the day. While waiting for the girls to come by her house for pizza and wine, she writes a letter to relieve some of the stress from what occurred.

This easily can be labeled as one of the worst days of my life. All I wanted was to meet my father. But instead, I meet his conniving wife who single-handedly ripped my family apart. She thought money would make me change my intentions.

I don't know how my mother even dealt with a man who has an evil family like that. I'm convinced my mother took all those drugs to avoid thinking of her. That lady is the devil. It absolutely makes no sense for me to be treated in such a way.

I can't wait for the girls to come over here with the pizza and wine. Lord knows I need it. I hope some way, somehow, the universe will allow me to meet him just one time.

I thought I had a lot of questions to ask him. What made him leave, did he ever love us? Questions about my mom, but now the only question I want to ask him is "Why?"

Why not stay no matter what you and my mother went through? He should have done that for us. He did not fight for us. He just allowed everything to go the way it did.

I'm tired of making all these confessions from my soul.

Ally

As soon as Ally finishes penning the last of the letter, she hears a knock at the door.

She opens the door, assuming it is the girls, and is surprised to see Alex standing there.

"Oh wow, I wasn't expecting you."

Alex smiles and says,

"Yeah, I know. I'm sorry to come here unannounced, but I wanted to make sure you were okay."

"Yeah, I'm okay. I'm actually expecting some friends or I would invite you in."

Alex says,

"Oh, I totally understand. I just saw how fast you stormed out of there and how angry you looked, and wanted to make sure everything was alright."

"I'm as good as I can be. Thank you for stopping by, that's really thoughtful of you."

"Any time. That's the least I can do. If you need anything, just let me know."

Before Alex can leave, the girls show up in the hallway. This makes Ally nervous and she starts to turn red. None of them really know about Alex, except for the time she told Sarah she was making dinner for him, and once when she mentioned him in conversation.

Alex smiles, seeing that Ally is nervous and says to her,

"I guess this is my cue. Take care, Ally."

"Bye, Alex."

Melinda sees him walking by, and before he even gets in the elevator, she is interrogating Ally.

"Alley, who was that?"

Alley, not wanting to say much,.

Alley tells Melinda,

"He's a friend."

Melinda says sarcastically,

"Right."

Janice says,

"Can we please come in and not stand here in the doorway? We have the pizza and Sarah has the wine."

Sarah and Janice move Melinda and Ally out of the way and rush to the couch so they can pick a television show to watch while eating.

As they munch on the pizza, Melinda asks,

"So, what's new? You only ask us to bring pizza and wine when you want a favor or you're going through something."

"I called you guys over to let you know that I met my grandmother on my father's side and his wife. The meeting did not go the way I planned."

The girls are interested to hear what happened and slide closer to Ally to hear her story.

"My grandmother is Mrs. Lee, and she told Alex, the guy you just saw, that she wanted to see me. Then when I got there, his wife was there too. Although what my grandmother said was true, she didn't say it so I could see my father; they tried to buy me off.

The girls are stunned and in disbelief that all this took place.

Janice says,

"I'm sorry that you're going through this. Is there anything we can do?"

"Yeah, if you guys can come by my mother's apartment so I can pack some of her things up for storage, I would really appreciate it."

Janice says,

"No problem, you know I'll be there."

Sarah adds,

"Me too."

Melinda shrugs her shoulders before saying,

"How else would I want to spend my Monday besides helping out a great pal."

Ally smiles,

"My thoughts exactly. I'm going to head to bed. I have a long day ahead of me. Lock the door when you guys leave."

Mom and Son

James uses the spare key he has to his mother's apartment and storms in screaming at her.

"What the hell are you doing? What did anyone ever do to you? Because of you and my soon-to-be-ex-wife's antics, I will not be seeing my daughters. I'm glad Ally smacked Robin. I wish her mother hadn't raised her to be so damned respectful, or else I would have prayed to God that she smacked you too."

His mother says,

"Why are you going off the deep end? If anything, I am doing you a favor. It may not come across that way, but I am protecting you. When you became

212

successful, you sent those girls money every month of their lives and didn't even see them."

James looks at his mother with disgust,

"And do you know what their mother did with the money I sent them?"

Mrs. Lee makes a smart remark,

"What? Used it for more drugs?"

"No, she never cashed the checks. She didn't want anything to do with me after she found out I was with Robin. You never liked her or my kids. Why is that?"

"Because you could have done better; she made you play house, made you drop out of college. Thank God for your father. He taught you about the business and found a way for you to make something of yourself."

"Let's be clear. That was my stepfather, and I'm grateful for the lessons he taught me. But you married that man for his money. You wouldn't know love if it hit you in the face. I'm through dealing with you and

Robin's bull. Both of you only care about money. Robin lied, said she was going to talk to you about getting the information on my daughter. Instead, you two use that information to push her away, to keep me from reconnecting with my daughters."

Mrs. Lee doesn't know what to say, and realizes she has made the biggest mistake of her life, as she truly treated her granddaughter horribly. Not wanting to think about it, she goes to the liquor cabinet, which has been locked for fifteen years. She keeps a bottle of whisky in there and starts to drink from the bottle, knowing she has lost her son because of her poor decision.

Before he walks out the door, James says,

"Mom, if you love me, you will fix this. Not on your time, but mine. I have a doctor's appointment tomorrow to find out if I'm able to have an operation for the tumor."

Mrs. Lee says nothing as he walks out of the apartment. All she hears is the sound of James' shoes walking on the red oak floor until the door slams shut. When she hears that, she flinches, as the sound shakes the floors of the entire penthouse.

James is sitting at his kitchen table, fuming, unable even to vent to his wife, because she is a major part of the problem. James decides to write a letter to blow off some steam, as he is afraid he'll get into a screaming match with Robin that might wake up his kids.

What a Sunday this was. I was so close to being able to see my daughter. I told their mother I would love her forever, and I lied. I began a relationship with another woman, and in doing so, I lost my two older daughters.

My two oldest daughters had nothing to do with my selfishness. I lied to Marisa. I remember her eyes like it was yesterday, when I told her I was going to the store and all she could say to me in her cute little voice was, "Daddy?" and I said "Yes," and the last words she said to me were "Can you please get me some candy." All I could do was smile and say, "Of course, baby."

Then I gave her a hug and a kiss on her forehead and haven't seen them since. I'm a disgrace as a father. I'm not even a weekend father. Those two girls motivated me to get my act together. I never had the opportunity to let them know they are the only reason for my success. They were in my thoughts every morning. When I didn't want to wake up, they were my source of energy.

I pray that somehow the universe will bring me back to my baby girls, Marisa and Ally.

Love, your dad,

The Apartment

Ally opens the door and takes a deep breath before walking into the apartment. Not even two months have passed since Ally and Janice walked into the apartment, and Ally saw her mother's feet dangling, and her head hanging down.

Ally looks into every part of the house, and has small glimpses of her childhood, and each lesson she learned growing up there.

In the living room, Ally remembers the wall where she and Marisa used to measure each other. She walks over to the wall and hears her sister's voice inside her head, and recalls the last time they checked one another's height. The pencil mark on the wall is faded now.

She then walks into her mother's bedroom and smiles as she pictures her mom and dad sitting on the bed while she and Marisa sat on the floor watching television and eating popcorn.

She hears a knock on the door and, a bit paranoid, says,

"Who's that?"

Sarah and Melinda both shout their names so she will know it is them.

Sarah says,

"It's me and Melinda. Who do you think it is? You asked us to come by to help and you can't even greet us?"

Ally lets them in and rolls her eyes before talking to Melinda and Sarah,

"Sorry, I was taking a walk down memory lane. Glad you guys can come and join me, although you're late.

Melinda says,

"The only reason we're late is because we needed to get some coffee. We knew you were not going to provide us with that, now were you?"

Sarah cuts into the conversation,

"Hey, where is Janice, and do you want a doughnut?"

Ally says,

"No thanks, and she should be coming in a few minutes. Let's start packing up the living room."

Ally gives directions to the girls, and Sarah starts packing books and photo albums in boxes to be shipped to Ally's house, while Melinda takes miscellaneous items and packs them to go to the storage unit where Ally has Marisa's belongings, as she could not get rid of anything that seemed to be important to Marisa.

Janice finally comes into the apartment twenty minutes after the girls started cleaning and organizing the living room.

"Hey, Ally, what do you need me to do?"

Ally gives Janice a hug, and says,

"I just need you to fill those boxes for me, and after you do that, we can clean out my mother's bedroom."

"Alright, no problem. How are you feeling being here and all?"

"I'd be lying if I said I still don't remember my mother or Marisa whenever I'm here."

Janice frowns, trying to think what to say,

"Keep your head up. It looks like Sarah and Melinda have the living room under control, so let's start with your mother's bedroom."

Ally starts to freak out a bit,

"I don't think I'm ready to go in there yet. I have too many memories of that room. I'm not ready to clear it. I just can't, Janice, I can't."

Janice grabs Ally by the shoulders and says as she looks straight into her face without flinching,

"Ally, the word 'can't' has been out of your vocabulary for a very long time, don't you forget that. You *can* go into your mother's room and you *will* remember the good moments when you look around. Take it all in. Because after today, you won't be coming back here. Take this moment to enjoy how far you have come in your life. You're the last one standing in your family and if your dad doesn't want to be a part of it, that's his loss. You completed the hard parts, surviving your sister's and mother's deaths. Your sister gave you the money, so now you can really live, and the only way you're going to do that is by going into your mother's room and officially letting her go."

Ally has tears flowing down her cheeks, and says,

"I don't know, but I'll try."

Ally slowly makes her way to her mother's bedroom, which still radiates the smell of Peruvian lilies, her mother's favorite flower.

Janice removes all of the clothes from the closet carefully, while Ally goes through the drawers in her mother's armoire. She sees a bulky accordion folder that is marked James' Letters. Curious about what it could be, Ally drops everything she is working on and screams loudly enough for Melinda and Sarah to hear her in the living room.

"Hey, come here for a second!"

Janice, already in the room, has her hands over her ears. Melinda and Sarah rush into the bedroom, as they think she was injured by the way she screamed.

Melinda says,

"What happened, what happened? Are you alright?"

"Yeah, I'm fine, I just want you all to be here before I open this."

The girls wonder what she is talking about, and ask her what it is. Ally then shows them the accordion folder with the label, "James' Letters."

Janice says,

"What, you think he wrote your mother letters?"

"I don't know. This is the first time I've seen this. I'm scared to open it. Can one of you do it for me?"

Melinda, not thinking what she's saying, replies,

"You better stop acting like a punk. This is not the S.A.T. This is your life. Now you're gonna open up that folder and see what's inside."

Janice says,

"I know that came out harsher than she meant it to. However, Melinda would not be Melinda if she did not speak her mind, and I have to agree with her. Put on your big girl pants and open it."

Sarah chimes in,

"I'm gonna have to agree with them too. Nothing could be worse than your grandmother treating you the way she did. All you have to do is open it and see what's inside."

Out voted, Ally opens the folder. She takes her time, opening it slowly, scared of what may appear, acting like it is destined to have or be bad news.

When she opens the folder, the first thing she notices are the dividers and sees that they all have a year on them, starting from the year her father left.

Ally puts her hand in the folder and takes out a stack of letters that her father wrote in that year alone. She glances at a few of them and starts to cry, as she realizes that her mother kept all these letters from her and Marisa.

Janice, seeing that Ally is distraught, and now deeply saddened, asks,

"What's wrong? What are those papers about?"

"They're letters my father wrote to me and Marisa. She kept them from us."

Janice says,

"Oh Ally, I am so sorry that you're just finding this out."

Ally dries her tears.

"Yeah, me too. There's one here that he wrote to her, and then there is one he wrote to me and Marisa."

Janice says,

"What did he write to your mother?"

Ally looks at the letter, takes a deep breath, and starts to read what James wrote to her mother.

Dear Janet,

I have no words for my decision. All I can tell you is that I love you and that I am sorry. I never intentionally meant to hurt you, and I never meant to cheat on you, but I could not handle coming home to you and your addiction.

I was not making any money and I used those women as an escape from the hell we created for our daughters. It's been two months since I saw Marisa and Ally, and I am begging you to arrange a date for me to see them.

I knocked on the door around a week ago, and I know you heard me, cause you told me never to come back. But Janet, it stopped being about us a long time ago. It's about our kids now, and I wish you would understand that.

I just want to let you know that my stepfather gave me an opportunity to change my life. He taught me about real estate. I just sold my first home, and will be sending you money shortly.

I love you and my daughters. Please let me have a relationship with them, I beg you. I can live with you not wanting to be with me, but I will never be okay if I can't speak to my daughters again. With my deepest regret for the way things have become,

Your first love, your first sweetheart, James

"At least you know that he wanted to see you," Janice says.

Everyone is at a loss for words and wishes they could say something to Ally, who stands silent for a minute, thinking about what she just read. Then, she sits on the bed and says,

"Here is the first letter he ever wrote to us."

Dear Marisa and Ally,

I know it's been sometime since we spoke, and I just want to let you know that I love you both and it was not

easy for daddy to go away. Your mother and I were not getting along. To make sure my beautiful girls could stay happy, I needed to leave.

Leaving had nothing to do with you girls. Daddy just made a big mistake that forced your mother to be mad at me, and she had every right to be so.

Marisa, I hope you are having a good time in your dance class. Ally, I hope you're eating all your vegetables. They will make you the smartest and strongest girl in the world.

Marisa, continue to do well in school, and remember that hard work will always prevail.

To my daughters, you are my world, and I love you both. I hope to get a letter from you soon. I love you more than I could ever show.

Love, Daddy

Ally skims through some of the other letters and sees that every letter after the first year that her father wrote contained a check.

Ally starts to smile, as she finds it impressive that her father sent a check every month until he knew she turned eighteen. She finds it even more impressive that her mother never cashed a single check.

Melinda asks,

"Why do you have a smile on your face when your mother kept you from knowing your dad?"

Janice slaps Melinda on the back of her head before saying,

"Why do you have to say it like that, stupid?"

Ally says,

"Don't call her stupid, Janice, that's just how she is. You have to expect that coming from her. She's always been that way."

Melinda asks,

"What do you mean?"

"You're insensitive. You don't think before you speak. That is what I mean, and the reason why I'm smiling is because my dad showed that he does love me by writing the letters and by the checks he sent. It shows me he has a heart and he actually feels guilty. But what really made me smile is that my mother was so strong willed. There were plenty of times we could have used the money, but she never cashed any of his checks. He even sent a check for a hundred thousand dollars, and she still was not impressed. Do you know how strong you have to be to turn down a hundred thousand dollars? You have to be pretty damned strong willed to say no to that much money. Gosh.

A light bulb went off after a minute of keeping the idea to herself, and she asked the girls what they thought about her latest idea.

"Hey, look, I think this might be his address on the check. What do you guys think?"

Janice looks at the check and says,

"That is definitely his address, but I think it's for work, not home."

Melinda says,

"Looks like we're going to have a special meeting with him tomorrow."

Sarah agrees,

"Sounds like a plan to me. What about you, Janice?"

Janice says,

"It's early enough to go now. What are we waiting for?"

Ally says,

"You all need to wait on me. I'm not ready to go today. We still have work to do here. We'll go tomorrow around nine. He should be in the office by then."

Clear Heart, Open Mind

*W*ho would have thought that so much would change in my life in the month since we got back from Japan? When I thought I was coming back to my mother just having an addiction, what I really saw was her feet dangling from the bathroom ceiling like a piece of strange fruit.

To go from thinking that my father never loved us to realizing that he actually does. I hope I find it in my heart to forgive him for being absent from my life. I know he has some great qualities, but the sad thing is that I don't remember them.

I only remember the feelings Marisa had growing up, because she was old enough to remember and tell me what he was like. Tomorrow I get to see him, and I'm eager to ask him every question I have, rather than read the letters he wrote and assume that he still has the same feelings for me and my sister.

I hope my sister's spirit is with me, because I have no idea how it will go. I just hope the feelings for me and Marisa that he wrote about in the letters have not changed much since the last letter he wrote to me.

Ally

Family Meeting

Ally is waiting for the girls to meet her in the lobby of the building where her father works. There is a Starbucks there where she is drinking a Café Mocha.

While surfing social media on her phone, she receives a text from Alex. The text instantly puts a happy smile on her face.

Alex texts:

"Can you stop thinking of how handsome I am. I would greatly appreciate it."

Ally replies:

"You are far from handsome. You did me a favor, so I just tried to let you know that you are greatly appreciated as well."

"Well, just wanted to text you and wish you a good morning."

"Thanks a lot. Have a great day, Alex, and maybe we'll talk soon."

"I'll take that 'maybe' as a guarantee."

"Maybe."

"Dinner tonight?"

"Maybe."

Finally the girls arrive.

Sarah says,

"Hey, Ally."

Melinda and Janice echo her greeting and both wave to Ally.

Janice says,

"Are you ready to handle business?"

"As ready as I'm going be."

Ally then walks to the security guard's desk, while the girls watch her.

"Hello, can I help you?"

"Yes, I have a meeting."

The guard does not look up at Ally, just wants to hear the name she requests.

Ally says nothing at first because she's anxious, then she croaks weakly,

"James Santos."

The security guard, unable really to hear Ally, says sharply,

"Speak up, please."

"James Santos."

"I don't see your name here. Is he expecting you?"

Ally lies,

"Yeah, he told me he was going to tell his secretary so she could put me down on the schedule. I guess they had a communication breakdown, because I was told I had a job interview at nine-thirty."

The security guard smiles and says,

"That's five minutes from now. I'm going to make an exception and let you go up."

The security guard prints out a temporary pass so Ally can take the elevator and head up to her father's office. She waves to the others as the doors close.

While on the elevator, she says the prayer her grandmother always said to her and Marisa when they were growing up.

Oh Lord, that you would bless us indeed, and enlarge my territory, that your hand will be with me and that you will keep me from evil. Therefore, I cannot cause any pain.

Amen

Ally is greeted by James' personal receptionist.

Ally asks her,

"Hi, can I please speak to James Santos?"

"Sure, who shall I say is here?"

Before Ally can say who she is, James walks out of his office with a file in his hand to ask his receptionist a question. He is stunned to see Ally.

James looks into Ally's eyes and drops the folder in his hand. Before his receptionist can say anything, James gives her specific instructions.

"Jill, cancel all my morning meetings."

"But, sir…"

"Sir nothing, cancel my meetings."

"Yes sir."

"And Jill?"

"Yes sir?"

"Say hello to my beautiful daughter."

Jill is shocked for a moment. She just sits in her chair and mumbles to herself to make sure she heard what James just told her, and after realizing what he said and having it register in her brain, she gets up and shakes Ally's hand.

"Hello, Miss Santos, can I get you anything? Water, coffee, a soda?"

"No thank you, Jill."

James walks to Ally and gives her a hug that is long overdue for both of them. James, not letting Ally out of his sight, walks her into his office where they both sit on a leather couch and begin to become reacquainted.

Ally tells him,

"I have so many questions for you that I don't even know where to start."

"I just want to tell you that I am sorry for all the hardships I caused you. I am truly and deeply sorry for what I put you and Marisa and your mother through."

"I feel like I have to forgive you. I had so much anger built up for so many years, and I thought it was entirely your fault for so many years, and then I came across all those letters you wrote and checks you sent, and put it together that my mother was keeping us away from you."

"I should have tried harder and, again, I am sorry for that. Your mother and I were in a dark place, trying to figure out our lives, and I'm sorry that we brought you along for the ride. Where is Marisa?"

Ally thought she was ready to talk about it, but at that moment, she knows she isn't. Ally looks into her purse and gives him the notebook that Marisa wrote in before she passed away. She turns to the page that she wrote to her friends to tell her she was going to die.

"I think you should read this."

James puts on his glasses to read the page Ally has turned to in Marisa's notebook.

Today feels like my last day on this earth. I hope I did what God had planned for me. I hope these letters will keep me in the memory of all my loved ones. I hope everyone and anyone who reads this will be inspired to live a better life than I did. I hope my best friends read this, and I hope my mother knows I forgive her, and I hope my sister can forgive me.

Mom, I love you, and I know you did your best to raise Ally and me. I know you meant well, even though your addiction limited you. I haven't been the best daughter either. I blamed you for Dad leaving us. I have the same level of patience, which is not saying much.

Ally, I love you so much. I'm sorry I couldn't raise you and the state intervened. Please understand that Mom really needed help, and I became emancipated, which was selfish of me. I wish I could tell you in person, but I do not have the strength to do so. Even though these may be my last words to everyone I care for, I still can't work up enough courage to tell you or anyone else of my feelings.

To Sarah, Melinda, and Janice, besides my sister, you three are my sisters. You guys treated me just the same after I told you about my illness. If my journal is confusing to you, it's because it is also confusing to me. Right now, I am going to break down everything you guys just read, from the trips we never went on, to where you can find the ticket.

I did win the lottery. When you turn to the last page of the book, you will see the key to the PO box and which post office to go to: retrieve the winning ticket with the rules that come along with it.

I went on this journey in my mind these last weeks, this journey of what would be the best way to leave this earth, and although I will never be able to do it physically, I hope you will visit the places I talked about. I want you all to pull a prank in every city, and I want you girls to find my sister, and have her take my place on this trip. I want her to know what life is like with women like you.

If there's one thing I want you all to remember, it is that time should not be taken for granted. I have written what I wish I had done during the last days of my life with the sisters I love. I felt it was more important to write this notebook describing what I wanted you to do in my memory. My dad always said I was lucky. I guess my winning proves that point. I'm sure there was a better chance of having cancer than of winning the lottery; I did both. Cancer was a blessing; it showed me that everything I needed was in front of me. I had loyal friends who stayed by my side. I found people who truly loved me. I wish I had met a man before I left this earth, but we can't have it all, and that's what I learned. Appreciate your journey and make an impact in your lives. I'm going through all this pain, which will make me appreciate heaven. Obviously, God knew exactly what he was doing, and for that, I am so grateful.

I love you all, and please never forget about me on your journey. Keep me in your hearts while God now has my spirit. I love you all.

Marisa

After reading the letter Marisa wrote in her notebook, James starts to cry.

"I'm so sorry. When did this happen?"

"Around two years ago. I received the news when I was in a group home."

"Wait, what? You were in a group home? What happened with your mother," James says, shocked to hear Ally say this.

Ally tries to find the words.

"Marisa emancipated herself and because of that, I became a ward of the state. There was a letter that said that if something was to happen to my mom, I would go to your mom, but thank God that never materialized. My mom became unfit due to her addiction at the time."

"That makes no sense. Neither Janet nor my mother ever said anything about this. How is Janet holding up?"

"She is the reason why I knew you still existed. She is the reason why I came here. I think you should read this too."

Ally hands him her mother's letter to her.

To my baby Girl,

I'm sorry. I know this is selfish of me, but why should I live as your grown baby?

The only thing that was significant was giving birth to you and your sister. You do not need me, no matter what you think.

I've really had a lot of emotional pain, and I don't even remember what I ate two hours ago. In case you don't know, I am in the early stages of Alzheimer's disease.

When Marisa died, part of me died with her, and no longer having a sound mind, there's nothing for me to enjoy in this world.

I don't want you to continue to take care of me because of my depression, because of my illness. So I leave you to find your own way.

I had this information for you. It's a month old now, but there was never a proper time to tell you. Your father contacted me, trying to get in touch with you.

In my phone book, you will see his contact information on a sticky note.

Just know your father loved you very much, but we had our issues. Please do not bear any ill will towards him.

Ally, I love you so much. Please continue to grow. You never needed me. You always found your way.

You became my mom when I should have made a better effort to be yours.

Love, Mom

"So, she is no longer here for you. I'm so sorry that you had to go through all of this. I wish I had known."

"The past is the past. What matters is that you are in my life now. I want to apologize for hitting Robin, and threatening Mrs. Lee. She is still my grandmother, and I could have acted better."

"They tried to sabotage us meeting, because I have cancer, and they want to make sure no one will be added to my will, and that I wouldn't be giving anything to anyone else. What I failed to tell them is that the cancer has been in remission. I received a call from my doctors a few months back."

"It's good to know that we may have time to do this again." Ally then smiles nervously.

James says,

"I want you come to my house for family dinner Sunday. I would love to introduce you to your brothers and sister, but only if you are comfortable with that."

Ally smiles,

"I would love that, but maybe you can come to my house."

A New Day

Janice calls Ally on Sunday.

"Hello, Ally. What do you have planned today?"

"James is going to introduce me to my younger siblings, the ones with his second wife."

"Not really wanting to call him dad yet?"

Ally smiles,

"No, I feel that should be something earned, not given. We'll see how dinner goes. They're supposed to be coming here soon."

"You're allowing them into your house?"

"Yeah, don't forget I smacked his wife?"

"Well, she deserved it."

"I agree. Let me get off the phone. I'm in the process of baking a cake."

"Okay. I won't hold you. Have a great time."

"I'll try."

After baking the cake, Ally orders Chinese food and after a while, she hears a knock on the door.

"Who is it?"

"It's James."

Ally takes a deep breath before opening the door.

With a bright smile, James takes a step in and hugs Ally so hard, he squeezes her like a sponge, and she starts gasping for air.

"I…can't…breathe."

"Oh, I'm sorry. I'm just really excited to have dinner with my daughter."

"Who are these two handsome guys and this lovely young lady?"

The first boy says,

"Hi, I'm James, and this is Jose."

The little girl pipes up,

"And I'm Mallory."

"Hey guys, are you hungry?"

They all say,

"Yes."

James Junior asks,

"Are you our sister?"

"Yes, I am."

"How come we're just finding out now that we have a big sister?"

Ally doesn't know what to say, and James steps in.

"It's my fault. I'll tell you guys a bit later. Go sit down. I know you've met my wife."

"Yes, I have. Hey, Robin, listen, I'm sorry…"

Before Ally can finish her sentence, Robin cuts her off.

"You should not be sorry. I deserved that smack. I'm sorry that I treated you the way I did. I know better, and I did wrong by you. I'm deeply sorry for my actions, and hope that from this day forward, we can have a better relationship."

Ally says,

"I think we can. I would love to do this more than just this one time. You guys are the only family I have left."

Robin says,

"I know our kids would love that, and I know James really wants to reconnect and be in your life."

James says,

"Let today be a new day."

Robin echoes,

"A new day."

Ally replies,

"Yes, a new day."

The Last Page

*T*he sun shines on my family every day. This has been one hell of a ride, from losing my sister to becoming a millionaire, to having my sister's friends take me into their sisterhood. And then, seeing my mother's body after she committed suicide.

Through all the struggles in my life, I never allowed myself to stay amongst the ashes. I always rose, the way a phoenix does.

It would be easy to blame my mom for not allowing Marisa and me and my father to reconnect. But I know everything happens for a reason. Situations that we don't understand are just seasons, they are the dark lessons that need to be learned. There is a blessing that comes from any dark moment.

Although I have lost family members, we all shine bright. This is our story. This is not just about Marisa, or me. This is about all of us, the Santos family.

My family and friends are the reason why I am the woman I am today. I will forgive my past, live in the moment, and love my future.

Ally

Acknowledgements

First and foremost, I want to thank God for blessing me with a great story to share with His world. Although I feel this is the end of the story of these characters, my journey as a writer will continue. I have many more stories to tell, and can't wait to share the art that God has entrusted to me. To my family and friends, I am nothing without the energy you give me. Thank you to all the readers of my work, as I am nothing without you. I hope this journey was as great for you as it was for me.

Love you all,
Brinton Woodall

Printed in the United States
By Bookmasters